RENEGADE

SPECIAL TACTICAL UNITS DIVISION, BOOK 3

SANDRA MARTON

RENEGADE

Special Tactical Units Division, Book 3
By Sandra Marton
Copyright 2016

First Print Edition
ISBN 9780997291537

Published by Sandra Marton
www.sandramarton.com
Published in the Untied States of America

1

It was a perfect California evening.

The sun had set a couple of hours ago and now a big ivory moon hung over the Pacific ocean.

Declan Sanchez's cottage was right on the beach. The cottage was pleasant and efficient during the day. At night, it could become the ideal bachelor pad, a perfect setting for a guy who could have beautiful women in his bed 24/7 if that was what he wanted.

Turn the lights down low. Open the French doors to the salt-scented breeze and the whisper of the surf. Have a bottle of rich-tasting merlot or a crisp pinot grigio ready to pour. Play something sexy and soft on the audio system.

Tonight, the wine was merlot. The music was by Coldplay. The scene was just right. So was the blonde in the living room. She had long legs, great curves, a spectacular face, and she'd made it crystal clear that she was eager to climb into Dec's bed.

In other words, everything was a go.

Everything but Dec, who stood in front of his bathroom sink, staring at himself in the mirror.

What the fuck was he doing? Not what he was supposed to be doing, that was for sure.

And that was crazy.

He was into hot sex with hot women. Had been, ever since he'd turned sixteen. He was thirty-one now and his feelings about sex and women had not changed.

Plus, women liked him. A lot.

There was nothing immodest in admitting it.

Dec was tall. Lean. Tightly muscled. His hair was brown, though women insisted on describing it as chestnut shot through with gold. His eyes were so dark they were almost black. It was an unusual combination, courtesy of a born-in-the-USA mother and a born-in-Colombia father. He had a square jaw and a nose that was—what had one woman called it? Assertive. That was the word. What it meant was that he'd broken it once, taking down a Taliban fighter in Iraq, and it had healed with a little bump below the bridge. It was a nice accompaniment to the scar that laced through one eyebrow, a souvenir of an equally stimulating encounter in the mountains of Afghanistan.

Being a STUD was an interesting job.

Dec knew he looked big and tough and, in the proper setting, intimidating. Hell, he *was* big and tough. And intimidating. He was supposed to be all those things. Walk into a bar, get dropped behind or even into an enemy encampment—he could handle anything that was waiting for him.

Dec groaned.

Anything but the blonde in the next room.

Okay.

Maybe he could rearrange the expression on his face. How about a smile? An arched eyebrow? Head tilted at an inquisitive angle?

"Fuck!"

He still looked as if he was waiting for a root canal instead of waiting to climb into bed with a hot, built-like-a-brick-shithouse babe who'd spent an hour on the dance floor doing everything but reaching into his pants.

Now it was time for more than that.

And he wasn't interested in delivering.

Jesus H. Christ, Sanchez, are you crazy?

He had to be.

Okay. Forget re-arranging his face. How about thinking positive thoughts? Meaningful thoughts.

Like, the blonde, naked.

Not just naked.

Naked and in his bed.

Naked, with her hair spread over the pillow, her arms reaching for him, her thighs wide apart...

"Dec?"

Dec jumped. She was right outside the door.

"Dec?" A light tap at the door. "You okay?"

"Yes. Fine." Dec cleared his throat. "I'll be out in a minute." Crap. Wasn't that a woman's line? "I mean, I just need another couple of seconds..." Man, this was going from bad to worse.

"How about if I wait in your bedroom?"

"No!" Shit. He'd damn near barked the word. A STUD instructor trying to terrify a class of newbies couldn't have done better. "Uh, I was thinking...It's a beautiful night. How about waiting for me out on the patio?"

"Well, sure. If that's what you want."

What he wanted was to open this door and find himself alone. Turn back time, erase having been at the Landing Zone. Or at least erase responding to her when she'd come over and asked him to dance, erase having been stupid enough to follow her onto the packed dance floor...

"Dec?"

The blonde was getting impatient. He couldn't blame her. A guy takes a woman home with him, then vanishes into the john...

"Coming," he said—and winced.

Bad choice of words. Coming was the last thing that would happen tonight. Yes, he needed sex. No, not with this woman. Not with any woman except for the one woman he'd never had sex with and would never see again and, goddammit, was that fucked up or was it fucked up?

"Lieutenant?"

Okay. This was not the time for gazing into his navel, it was the time for a diversion, something to save his ass, fast. *Think, Sanchez. Think...*

And just that quickly, he had the solution to the problem.

Dec flushed the toilet that didn't need flushing. Anything for a way to cover the sound of a phone call. He got his iPhone out of the pocket of his jeans, hit a button and muttered "Come on, come on, come on," while the number he'd called rang and rang and...

"Sanchez?"

Finally. The voice he needed was in his ear. Dec expelled a huge breath. "Romano."

"What's doin', dude? You only left here half an hour ago." Nick Romano chuckled. "You inviting me over to share?"

Crap. The toilet had stopped flushing. No sound cover. Dec turned on the water in the sink.

"Call me," he hissed.

"What?"

"I said..."

"Dude, between you whispering and AC-DC going full blast here, I can't hear a thing you're sayin'."

Dec stepped into the stall shower and slid the door closed.

"I said, call me."

"Call you what?"

"Jesus, Romano, this is no time for games. Call me. Wait a couple of minutes and then call."

"You want me to phone you."

"Yes."

Nick gave a low, wicked laugh. "The blonde needs to hear the phone ring to get off?"

"Dammit, this isn't funny. Give it two minutes. Then call. You got that?"

"Got it. And you owe me a full explanation. Details, from start to finish. Deal?"

"Deal," Dec said through his teeth, and disconnected.

Carefully, wincing at the slight sound the glass door made as he slid it open, he stepped from the shower stall, turned off the water in the sink and looked in the mirror. His short-cropped was curling at the ends, thanks to the humidity the running water had created. Dec grabbed a hand towel from the rack and rubbed it over his face and head, then checked his reflection again. He looked okay. Not sweaty, even though sweaty was how he felt.

What he *did* look was grim.

His mouth was a thin, tight line. The scar that slashed through his eyebrow stood out in stark relief.

"Did you get that killing somebody?" Blondie had asked breathlessly, once they were alone.

Dec ground his teeth together.

He should have turned her around right then and marched her outside. He hated women who asked crap like that. Plus, by then he'd already been asking himself what the hell he was doing, picking up a woman, bringing her home, when he had every reason to know it would not go well because he'd already been there, done that before in the last few weeks. Twice. Okay. Three times, if you were keeping count, and...

And, when was Romano going to...

The opening chords of *Born in the USA.* blasted out of his iPhone. Dec pumped his fist in the air, put what he hoped was a neutral look on his face, stepped out of the bathroom and walked briskly to the open French doors. Once he was on the patio, he accepted the call and said a brisk "Sanchez here."

"Okay," Romano replied. "It's me. What now?"

The blonde was sitting on one of the chaise longues. Her skirt was hiked to the tops of her thighs, her short cropped top had somehow grown even shorter. Her legs were crossed and a spike-heel sandal dangled from the scarlet-painted toes of one foot.

Dec looked at her and raised his eyebrows. *One second*, he mouthed, and then he said a brisk "Yessir" into the phone.

"Yessir, my ass," Romano growled. "What's the deal?"

""Yessir. I understand."

"Aha," Romano said. "The blonde isn't to your liking after all. Is that it?"

"That is correct. Sir."

"In that case, why not tell her you just won an all-expenses-paid trip to the Land of A Thousand Scorpions."

"Tonight, sir?"

"Deluxe accommodations at the SandSquat Hilton."

"Yessir. I hear you."

"Your trip includes all the activities the SandSquat Hilton offers. Rat races. Camel spider derbies. Various hunting options with your choice of weapons, everything from the handy-dandy Colt M4A1 assault rifle to, if you prefer, the ever popular HK MP7."

Dec felt his lips twitch.

Blondie's eyebrows rose.

He swung away from her. "That's very interesting sir."

"So let me know when you've heard enough, my man, because a bunch of us have a bet goin' here at the LZ about what the fuck is going on."

"Right now, sir? Because if it can wait just an hour or so..."

"Some of us figure Blondie's decided not to come across."

"That would be impossible, sir," Dec said.

Nick snorted. "You have an attitude problem, Sanchez."

"No sir. I am simply being truthful."

"Truthful, huh? Well, the majority says you're using me to lose Blondie. So be truthful, dude. Is that what's going down?"

What the hell. Romano would figure out the truth soon enough. "That would be an affirmative, sir."

Romano sighed. "Man, you are whacko."

"You're probably right, sir. But that's how it is."

"Mooning like a schoolboy over some babe..."

"Ten minutes, Captain," Dec said, his voice going flat and cold. "I'll see you then."

He ended the call and looked at the blonde.

She was sitting straight up. Her tiny skirt had inched even higher. An open bottle of ale was on the small table beside her. Apparently, she'd helped herself to it while he was hiding in the bathroom. Eyes on his, she tilted her head back, tilted the bottle up, and encircled the head of it with her lips.

Dec's cock rose in instant salute. It was reassuring to know his body parts were still working. For a couple of seconds he even reconsidered his plans.

The blonde was good looking. Better than good. Big blue eyes. Long platinum hair. Tits any man in his right mind would want to taste and touch...

A face swam into his mind.

Hazel eyes. A straight fall of lush brown hair shot through with gold. A delicate mouth, breasts he had only once tasted and barely touched except in endless dreams...

"What's happening, baby?" the blonde said.

Dec cleared his throat. "That was my commanding officer."

"And?"

"And, I'm afraid it's bad news."

Blondie's eyes narrowed. "Meaning?"

"Meaning, we're gonna have to cancel the rest of the evening. I'm really sorry, but—"

"The hell you are!"

"What's that supposed to mean?"

The blonde slammed the bottle of ale on the table and shot to her feet. "My girlfriends warned me about you."

Dec stared at her. "They what?"

"Hot-looking, they said. Nice line of BS, they said." She strode towards him. "Dances good, they said. Rub up against him on the dance floor, he'll get hard as a rock."

Jesus. Dec could feel his face start to burn.

"Listen, Susy—"

"It's Lucy," she snapped. "And what I should have done was listen to my friends. He'll take you some-place, they said, your motel room or maybe his place on the beach—and just before things start to happen, he'll come up with an excuse. A sick pal. An appoint-ment he forgot." She paused. "A call from his CO."

Shit. Had he done the call thing before? Yeah. He had. That time, he'd sneaked out on the patio and phoned Chay Olivieri.

"Susy. I mean, Lucy. I'm sorry. I just—"

She swept past him. He went after her.

"I'll drive you home."

"I followed you here in my car, remember?"

Of course she had. What now? What more could he say or do? He'd treated her badly. Hell, he'd treated a lot of women badly lately. It hadn't been deliberate. It was just that he couldn't fuck any of them when Annie was in his head.

And she was there, all the time.

The blonde yanked open the front door and strode across the porch to the steps.

"Lucy?"

She spun towards him. "What?"

"I need you to know..." Dec swallowed hard. "The thing is, it isn't you. It's me."

She laughed. Laughed! He knew his face must have gone even redder.

"That line's so old it has whiskers, Lieutenant. Why not try for the truth? You just can't get it up when it's time for action."

"No! It isn't that. I mean—"

Too late. She was inside her car, foot to the pedal, burning rubber as she made a U-turn and headed for the road.

Dammit.

She hadn't waited to hear him out...But what would he have said? *I can get a hard-on okay. I just can't imagine following through with you.*

Oh yeah. That would have been perfect. Just what a woman wanted to hear. Something to cap off the evening.

Man, he was a mess.

Dec sank down on the top porch step, leaned back on his elbows and stretched out his long legs.

The quiet of the night enveloped him.

He loved it here. Not so much the cottage, though it was handsome. What he loved was the endless beach. The infinite sea. Damn if he didn't sound like some half-baked poet, but it was the truth. He'd grown up in New Mexico. On a patch of land in the middle of nowhere. Desert. Scrub. And, in the distance, jagged mountain peaks against a pure blue sky.

It had been a long journey from that part of his life to where he was today.

He got to his feet and began walking, kicking the gravel as he made his way slowly across the parking lot.

He'd made an ass of himself with the blonde.

But he'd been a bigger fool with Annie Stanton.

Annie, studying for her Master's in Computer Engineering at UC Santa Barbara. Or so she'd claimed.

Annie, of the soft voice and topaz eyes. Annie, whose taste he would never forget. Annie, who he had never, not even once, made love to.

Forget making love.

What he'd never done was fuck her. A man didn't make love to a scheming, lying, cock-teaser. He fucked her—except, gullible idiot that he was, he'd never fucked her.

They'd come close.

His hands under her T-shirt. Her breasts, small and perfect against his palms. Her nipples, sweet as honey, against his tongue...

Christ!

He was hard as a rock and, goddammit, not in the mood to jerk himself off like some pathetic teenager. He'd done far too much of that lately and he wasn't a kid, he was a man.

Dec strode through the lot towards the darkness where the meadow began. Stopped. Turned. Strode back to his cottage. Went up the steps, across the porch, through the living room, out the French doors and onto the beach.

The beach was where he'd met Annie Stanton.

He'd been lying in a canvas hammock, chilling after getting back from the kind of mission that made you want to kiss the ground when you stepped off the transport that bought you home, listening to the whoosh of the surf and the cries of the gulls and hoping those sounds would crowd out the other sounds in your head, when something swooped past. Not a gull. Maybe an osprey.

He'd turned his head to check...And saw her instead. Annie, except he didn't know her name then. Not that he'd ever really known it, he thought, his mouth flattening into a thin line. She'd been standing ankle-deep in the frothing surf, a delicately-built brunette wearing a simple one-piece swimsuit.

Unusual, he'd thought.

In Santa Barbara, especially within five or six miles of the STUD base at Camp Condor, bikinis were what all the women wore. And they travelled in packs. Kitten packs, some of the guys called them. Lots of giggling, lots of T-and-A, all for the benefit of Condor and its retinue of hard-bodied, maybe-just-a-little-dangerous Special Ops warriors.

Dec had wondered what this modestly dressed woman was doing on what he thought of as his beach.

A middle-aged tourist, he'd decided, who'd wandered away from the usual tourist haunts. It was a little surprising because even though the law said that beaches weren't private property, this one pretty much was. The string of cottages was about it in both directions. There were no bars nearby. No shops. Plus, the tides were too strong for most swimmers.

The woman's back was to him. She was looking out to sea. And, yeah, she was delicate-looking. Petite was maybe the better word—five three, five four, with lustrous brown hair streaming down her back.

His gaze had dropped lower.

Maybe she wasn't middle-aged. She was slender, but she had a sweetly rounded ass. Nicely curved hips. Long legs. He wondered if she looked as good from the front as from the back.

Only one way to find out.

He'd swung his legs out of the hammock and sauntered across the sand towards her. When he was five, six feet away, he cleared his throat and said, "Hi."

She'd spun towards him, mouth open, eyes wide with fear, one hand clapped over her heart.

Shit. He'd startled her.

When he was twelve or thirteen he'd found a small songbird—a wren, he'd later found out. The wren hadn't been visibly hurt, but something had surely damaged it. It had stared up at him, wide-eyed, heart visibly beating in its breast. Dec had bent down, carefully picked it up and and held it until it was recovered enough to fly away.

Would this woman fly away too?

Crazy, but he hoped she wouldn't.

"Sorry," he'd said. "I didn't mean to startle you."

"No. You didn't. I mean—you did. Perhaps a little."

Her English was perfect, but he could detect the faintest accent. French? Not French. Something a little more exotic.

"See any dolphins yet?"

"Dolphins?"

"I figure you're looking for them They come to this stretch of water very often. It's the wrong season for Grey whales and too late for Blues or Humpbacks, but the dolphins are almost always a sure bet."

"I haven't actually been looking for anything in particular. I just—I found this place last week. I love how quiet it is."

So she'd come here while he was in Iraq.

He'd nodded. "Yeah. It is."

"And the ocean... It looks so peaceful."

Dec had thought of what swam beneath the blue surface of the Pacific: sharks, Morays, things that stalked and hunted and killed.

"Looks can be deceptive," he'd said.

Crap. His back-from-the-desert bitterness had hit the wrong note. She went from looking startled to looking wary.

"I meant," he'd added quickly, "there are some strong currents off this beach. You shouldn't swim here alone."

"Oh. Oh, I didn't come to swim. I'm just walking, that's all."

Her gaze had softened. Man, her eyes were unusual. Not brown. Not green. Hazel? No. Topaz was more accurate. Yeah. That's what they were. A rich, deep topaz set in an exquisite oval face. The rest of her was exquisite, too. Gently rounded breasts, a slender waist...

Suddenly, he'd realized he was staring. And she was blushing. And, like the wren, getting ready to fly.

Dammit, he was an idiot.

"Well," she'd said, "it's been nice meeting you, but I have to—"

"We haven't met," he'd said quickly, holding out his hand. "I'm Dec. Declan Sanchez."

She'd hesitated. Then she'd put her hand in his. He could still recall the electric shock that had hummed through him at her touch.

"Oh," she'd said, laughing a little.

Could something so simple tell you that your world was about to change?

Because it had. *She* had changed it. Forever. It was still changed, even now, months later, months since he'd met her, weeks since he'd discovered the depth of her lies, her deception...

A bright beam of light swept over the night-black beach. Dec swung around, threw up his hand against the blinding glare.

"Who's there?"

"Me. Nick. For crissake, dude, it's as dark as the inside of a heifer out here. Didn't you ever hear of electricity?"

"What the fuck would you know about heifers?" Declan said, laughing as Romano came towards him.

Romano, who had grown up in Brooklyn, laughed along with him.

"It's what a guy I went through BUD/S with used to say. And he would have known for sure. I mean, he was from flyover country." Nick reached Dec and jerked his thumb over his shoulder, back towards the cottage. "Checked out the territory. Saw it was clear of blondes."

"Yeah." Dec cleared his throat. "Dude. Thanks for bailing me out."

"Hey," Nick said, "what're friends for if not to do a little bailing every now and then?"

"Yeah," Dec said again. "See, the thing is—"

"The thing is," Nick said, "by the time we get, Olivieri will have eaten all the pizza, Sullivan will have polished off the beer, Maguire will be checkin' for hidden stashes of chocolate, and Spanos will be emptying your refrigerator."

"The whole unit's here?"

"You got it."

"And you brought pizza?"

"Comfort food. Of course."

Dec felt his throat constrict. "Dude. I don't know what to—""

Nick clapped Dec on the shoulder. "We don't wanna starve to death or die of thirst, we'd better get our asses moving."

"Yeah. Right." Dec hesitated. "Nick?"

"You try thanking anybody, dude, we'll take you for every dime you've got when we sit down to play poker."

Dec nodded. Smiled. Thanking these guys, these brothers-in-arms who stood up for each other, just wasn't done. They were family. They were always there for each other. They could count on each other the way he'd once stupidly imagined he could count on a woman...

Hell. Why go back to that? It was old shit, gone and best forgotten.

"Finally," Danny Sullivan said when Nick and Dec reached the patio. "Just when we were afraid the broccoli and tofu were gettin' cold."

Everybody laughed. And life was okay again...

Until an hour later, when all their smartphones

went off at once. The laughter, the sounds of cards hitting Dec's kitchen table, died. The men of STUD Unit One exchanged quick, tight glances as each reached for his phone.

"You guys together?"

It was the voice of their CO, Captain James Black.

Six "yessirs" echoed through the room.

"Sanchez?"

Dec automatically shot to his feet. "Sir."

"Put me on speakerphone. The rest of you, shut off your phones and listen."

Five phones were turned off.

"Everybody hear me, loud and clear?"

Six more "yessirs" filled the room.

"I want you all at base in thirty minutes."

Thirty minutes? When they'd just returned to the State forty-eight hours ago? The men looked at each other even as they pushed back from the table.

"Thirty minutes," James Black warned. "You're shipping out at zero three hundred."

"Sir," six voices snapped.

"Details when you get to Condor."

2

Twenty eight minutes later, the members of STUD One stood at attention in their CO's office.

"At ease," he said, and the men relaxed. "I'm sure you're wondering why you're heading out so quickly after what we can all agree was an, um, an interesting mission."

A faint sound of laughter.

"I won't bullshit you. This is going to be tough. I know, they always are—but this time, the rules will be a little different. You're be going in with minimal backup. If you're caught or captured—"

The men looked puzzled. There was nothing different in that. They'd gone this route before. If they were caught or captured, they'd be on their own. If you were a STUD, that was often how it went.

"What's different is that this job, more than most, has big—and I do mean big—international complications. Stein will brief you in greater depth in a couple of minutes. For now..." Black switched on a computer. A map appeared on a large monitor. At first, it could have been a map of anyplace in the middle east.

He jiggled the keys.

The view narrowed. Mountains. Deserts. Borders. Turkey. Syria. Iraq.

The view narrowed again. Dec stared at a dot that was its focal point. He could hear the sudden thud-thud of his heart.

"This, gentlemen," Black said, "is the kingdom of Qaram. It's small, rich in natural resources—everything but oil. And, and though it is considered a U.S. ally, for some time now, that allegiance has been less than solid." He paused. "Still, it is, as I said, an ally. And now, an incident of some importance has taken place that directly affects Qaram—and, by extension, us."

An incident.

Dec tore his gaze from the map and looked at his commanding officer. In Special Ops talk, an incident was not good. It was a term that covered anything from hostage-taking to plunder, rape and murder.

"A diplomatic party travelling from Qaram to the neighboring kingdom of Tharsalonia was attacked. Some of the group are dead. The rest are being held hostage."

Black touched the keyboard.

Click.

A new image appeared. Video, this time, of a man on his knees.

"Shit," someone whispered.

A pistol was pressed to the back of his head.

An off-screen voice spoke in accented English. "I am the Deliverer. I bring what Fate has decreed."

The pistol fired. Blood, bone and bits of flesh filled the screen.

"As you can see," Black said calmly, "the situation is deteriorating at a rapid pace."

Another click. A man's face. Resolute expression, but a large bruise on his forehead.

"The American ambassador to Qaram. He's a member of the party that was attacked."

Click. Another photo, this time of a woman. Middle-aged. Clearly terrified.

"The ambassador's wife."

Click. A guy in his thirties, bloodied mouth, cold eyes.

"An undersecretary from our Embassy."

"You mean, one of our spooks," said Sullivan.

"If we had spooks," Black said, straight-faced, "yeah, this guy probably would have been one of them."

Would have been. Would have been...

"Shit," somebody said. "The guy who was executed?"

Black nodded. "Yeah. That was him."

A final click. A final photo. Soft curses, and five heads swung towards Dec.

Dec looked like a man who'd just been struck by lightning.

That was sure as hell how he felt, because that final

photo...That photo was of Annie. Annie, covered head to toe in a voluminous hooded robe, her face dirt-smeared.

Dec felt the room tilt.

"Sanchez? I believe you know this woman."

Dec tore his gaze from the picture. "Yessir," he said hoarsely.

Black looked at the other men. "I think you all know her. Correct?"

Five voices mumbled their agreement.

"As Annie Stanton," Black said. "But, as we all know now, she is not Annie Stanton, she is Princess Anoushka, the daughter of the former king of Qaram, and the niece of its current ruler, King Cyrus."

Dec could hear the drone of his CO's voice, but all he could think about was Annie. Annie, laughing up at him. Annie, in his arms. Annie, trembling as he caressed her...

Olivieri jabbed an elbow into Dec's side.

"Sanchez?" Black said. "Are you with me?"

Dec swallowed hard and shot to full attention. "Yessir."

Black gave him a long, careful look. Then he turned that same look on the rest of Unit One.

"As I was saying, the woman is at the center of this situation."

Click. Another photo came onscreen. It showed a domed building backed by high mountains. Long black limos were parked in a circular driveway.

People were grouped in the driveway.

A couple of dozen ramrod-straight soldiers in fancy uniforms. The Embassy spook. The American ambassador and his wife. Half a dozen women in long dark robes.

And Annie.

Correction.

The Princess Anoushka, standing in the center of the group of women, her expression grim, her chin uplifted, the light of defiance shining in her topaz eyes.

"It's a wedding party," Black said. "The princess was traveling to Tharsalonia, where she was to marry the Tharsalonian king. Halfway there, they were attacked by a group of bandits who like to think of themselves as liberators. They're not. They're killers."

Dec heard a roaring in his ears.

Annie, on her way to her wedding. Annie, pledging herself to another man. Annie, his Annie...

Except she had never been his Annie. She'd never been a woman named Annie at all.

For reasons he knew he would never comprehend, she'd chosen him to take part in a game. And when she'd grown bored, she'd walked away.

No warning. No explanation, not even when he'd run into her at the wedding of Chay Olivieri and Bianca Wilde .

That was the day Dec had learned that Annie Stanton, grad student in computers, was really Princess Anoushka, daughter of the dead king of Qaram.

"Why didn't you tell me?" he'd said.

Her answer had been meaningless.

"You never asked," she'd replied.

Yeah. Right. He never had. Shit, why would he have asked? What would he have said? *Are you really who you say you are?* Yes, that would sure as hell be a question a guy would ask of a woman he'd been—he'd been becoming fond of.

Dec's jaw tightened.

Okay.

No problem.

He'd survived her disappearance from his life. The truth of her identity. Now he'd found out she was getting married. So what? And so what if she'd never wanted to talk about anything that even hinted at permanency...

They were all staring at him.

His CO. Andy Stein, the guy who generally gave briefings before missions. Sullivan and Olivieri, Spanos and Maguire and Romano, the men who were his brothers. His family.

These were the people who mattered, not some woman who'd passed herself off as the epitome of truth and innocence when all along she'd been a goddamn liar.

He had no feelings for her. None. He hadn't been good enough for her? Well, no. Not when it turned out she was royalty.

Big fucking deal.

She had her life. He had his. And his life was right here, with these people, in the room.

He drew a deep breath and said, as if Black's news had been no more earth-shaking than a weather report, "And we're to intervene."

Black's grim expression softened.

"Yes." He paused. "Sanchez. I understand you had a fairly close relationship with her."

"We knew each other, yessir."

"I'm designating you Alpha on this mission. If you have a problem with that, speak up now."

"No problem at all, sir," Dec said crisply.

"Good. Excellent. I didn't think you would. Stein? Take over."

Andy Stein adjusted his horn-rimmed glasses as he got to his feet.

"Okay, guys. Here are the basics."

He gave them longitude. Latitude. Weather, now and for the next few days, including the reminder that weather in the Copper Mountains was never really that predictable. He told them how and where they'd be inserted, how and where they'd be extracted.

Then he paused.

"You'll have some advantage here, Sanchez," he said. "Because you know the princess. She'll be predisposed to trust you."

Dec didn't respond. *Trust* wasn't a word he'd use in talking about the situation between him and the Royal Princess of Qaram.

"See," Stein said, "the thing is, she'll probably want to do what she thinks is best for her country. For Qaram. For us, that's a secondary issue. We want what's best for the three remaining Americans." He paused. "And for our own international interests."

"Wait a minute," Dec said. "The captain said there

were four Americans to begin with. How'd he reach that number? The ambassador and his wife. The embassy guy, but he's dead. By my count, there were three to start, and now we're down to two."

"Technically, there were four. Seems the princess has dual citizenship. Her father was Qarami, but her mother was born in Connecticut."

Dec's mouth thinned. What else hadn't he known about Annie Stanton?

"Has there been a ransom demand?"

Stein took off his glasses, blew on the lenses, polished them against the front of his shirt, then plopped the glasses on and pushed them up the bridge of his nose.

"Yes. But meeting it wouldn't be in our interest."

Dec nodded. "What do they want? Arms? Planes? Drones? Good old USA dollars?"

"Dollars for the ambassador and his wife. But for the the princess..." Stein hesitated. "They won't talk ransom. "

"Because?"

"Because they want to use her for political leverage."

"How?"

Stein bent over the computer and touched a couple of keys. The photo of the Embassy guy being executed appeared onscreen.

"The shooter, the guy who calls himself the Deliverer—Well, he isn't one of the bandits that captured the bridal party."

Dec got a bad, bad feeling. "Then who is he?"

A bearded, narrow face filled the screen. The eyes were cold, filled with evil.

"Fuck," somebody said.

They were looking at Altair Amjad, the leader of one of the most vicious terrorist groups on the planet.

3

Her Royal Highness, Princess Anoushka of Qaram, the woman who had once been Annie Stanton, sat shivering on the dirt floor of a wooden shed high in the mountainous no-man's-land that stretched for miles along the border between Qaram and its neighbor, Tharsalonia.

She was hungry, thirsty, and worn out.

Except for a cup of rancid-tasting water and a greasy glob of something that might have been goat, she hadn't had anything to eat or drink in the two days since she'd been captured. Dehydration, lack of food and her useless struggles to break free of the handcuff that shackled her to a wooden post had finally exhausted her.

She was also angry as hell—and even in her present state, she almost laughed at the irony of that phrase because it was surely not one a demure, obedient Qarami princess would ever use.

The thing was, she was neither demure or obedient, and she had long ago stopped thinking of herself as a Qarami princess.

She was Annie Stanton, which mean that instead of sitting here in subservient defeat, she was wracking her brain in an effort to come up with an escape plan —not easy to do when you couldn't focus all that well thanks to the lack of food and water.

Thanks to the cold.

The cold, the fact that she was shivering, that her teeth were banging together, worried her. She knew how debilitating it could be, that it could make it hard to think straight, that it could steal what little energy reserves she had left.

Then she would never escape—and no, she was not going to even consider that possibility.

A gust of wind sent its chilly fingers clawing through the cracks in the shed.

Annie used her free hand to draw her tattered silk gown around her.

It was all she had.

She'd been wearing it beneath a hooded cashmere cloak—the proper outfit for a bride, one of her so-called ladies-in-waiting had said—but it had been torn off her when she'd tried to fight against the rough hands of her captors as they'd dragged her from her limousine.

Her limousine.

As if anything to do with what her uncle had put in motion today was connected to her. And, yeah, that was the good news. That she was chained up in a shed while a bunch of outlaws drank themselves into a stupor meant that at least his horrible plans for her had suffered a setback.

But that was all it was. A setback, unless she found a way to escape these men, these mountains, this part of the world.

"Dammit," Annie said, and jerked against the handcuff for maybe the hundredth time.

Getting free of the cuff was impossible. She'd tugged and pulled, she'd banged her wrist against the post. She'd even chewed on the disgusting piece of fatty whatever one of he laughing captors had called food, trying not to gag until she had a mouthful of the slimy stuff. Then she'd licked her cuffed wrist until it was slippery as she could make it and she'd tried to work herself free.

Tried for what had seemed forever.

What she'd ended up with were cuts and bruises, but her wrist remained trapped.

Trapped, same as she was trapped.

She could stand or sit, but that was it. She was at the mercy of those who'd captured her, even when it came to emptying her bladder. Twice, a woman with missing teeth and a milky eye had wrapped a rope around Annie's neck, unlocked the handcuff from the post, and led her to a filthy bucket behind the small building.

The first time, Annie had backed away in disgust.

The second, she'd been desperate enough to use it.

That had made the woman cackle with laughter.

The wife of the American ambassador had received the same treatment, but Annie had no idea how she'd dealt with it. The ambassador's wife hadn't said a word, not since their capture. She was roped, not cuffed, to a ring in the opposite wall. Annie had eyed the arrangement with longing. The wall looked as if a stiff breeze might knock it down. If they'd shackled her the way they'd shackled the ambassador's wife, she was sure she could have broken free by now.

She'd whispered to the ambassador's wife, urged her to give it a try, but the woman didn't talk, didn't even make eye contact. She simply lay on her side, knees drawn up under her chin, and stared blankly into space.

After a while, Annie had switched tactics.

"Can you just get to the door and maybe crack it open enough to peek outside?"

No response.

"How many men did you count when they took you out to pee? I think I saw twenty."

Nothing.

Annie had stopped asking questions. She knew she'd have to rely on herself and she did a quick tally.

Thirty bandits. Maybe half a dozen more.

Her party had numbered thirty-eight when they left the palace in Qaram. Eight had died in the first furious minutes of the ambush. Four Royal Guardsmen. Three Qarami council ministers. One of her ladies-in-waiting.

Annie leaned back against the wall.

Such a fanciful name for female guards loyal to her uncle, but her uncle was good at that. At making evil things seem like good ones.

This wedding, for instance. As far as the world knew, she was a happy princess on her way to a fairy-tale wedding to her prince.

Annie shuddered.

The reality was that she'd been on her way to marriage to a man who agreed with her uncle that the world had been a better place when women were kept in a state of subjugation.

"Barefoot in the winter and pregnant in the summer," her uncle had said, laughing uproariously at the ugly old joke.

She'd been lost in those thoughts when half a dozen vehicles came tearing into the clearing when the Qarami party had stopped because of a flat tire.

Four Guardsmen had died then. At least that many, based on the sounds of gunfire, had died right here a couple of hours ago.

Annie had sat crouched in the semi-darkness of the shed, her hands over her ears in a useless attempt to drown out the screams and gunfire—although the next sounds had been worse.

The sounds of men roaring with laughter.

After that, there'd been silence, which was almost as bad as the screaming.

She tried not to think about what would happen next.

Instead, she thought about ways to escape.

About what was happening away from this terrible place.

Was there a rescue party coming? Would her uncle pay whatever ransom was asked for her, because surely this was about ransom? Or would he write her off as a deal gone bad?

After all, that was what she was.

A deal. Part of one, anyway. She, plus several million dollars, and the king of Tharsalonia would not interfere in her uncle's brutal expansionist plans for Qaram.

Annie groaned and lay her head back against the wall.

Every part of her ached. From the cold. From struggling with her captors and—*Be honest, Annie*—from fear.

Was death to be her fate as well?

What had awaited her—marriage to the king of Tharsalonia—would have been a kind of living death anyway.

Tears stung her eyes. She blinked them back. She wasn't going to give in to defeat. The trick was to keep her mind occupied. To think about good things, not bad.

This place—the shed—was ugly. It stunk of goats and chickens and of her captors, but she knew that the Copper Mountains themselves smelled of green growing things. Of flowers. Of sunshine. As a little girl, she'd spent summers in these mountains with her parents.

Her throat constricted.

Oh, how she'd loved them. Her beautiful mother, who'd given up the charmed life of an American debutante to become the wife of a handsome king determined to lead his people forward. Her loving father, who'd defied tradition by raising his daughter to be strong and independent.

"I am so proud of you, Anoushka," he'd said when she'd graduated from Oxford University, and he'd beamed with happiness when she'd enrolled in graduate courses at the University of California. He'd understood and supported her decision to do it under the name Anne Stanton—a combination of her mother's middle and maiden names—because she'd wanted to avoid the kind of publicity she'd run into at Oxford.

Annie's mouth trembled.

She remembered, too, the call a year later from her father's senior advisor, telling her of the plane crash that had taken her father's life as well as her mother's.

"I'll be on the next flight home," she'd said, sobbing.

"No!" the senior advisor had said, and then he'd told her that she could not return, not even for the funeral.

Her uncle Cyrus-—her father's younger brother— had immediately seized control of the governing council.

"He is intent on undoing all the good work of your father, Princess. If you return home, he will imprison you. You must stay away until we are powerful enough to oust him. He does not know the name and identity you have been using, and he must not learn it. Do you understand?"

Annie had understood all too well.

She had been raised in a royal court filled with the intrigue that accompanied two differing factions, one determined to keep the kingdom mired in the past, the other determined to bring it into the twenty-first century.

And so she'd stayed in America, alone and lonely, and devastated by grief...

Until, by chance, she took a walk along a windy stretch of beach and met a man. An amazing man.

"Declan," she whispered.

No. This wasn't the time to think about him. How she had hurt him, wounded him...

Tears spilled down her cheeks.

Declan. Her beautiful, proud lover.

Except, they'd never made love. Not really.

She had slept in his arms. Kissed him. Oh, those kisses! Gentle at first. Then more demanding More exciting. Her mouth had opened to his. Tasted his heat. His passion.

And that one time, that one incredible time, his hands and mouth on her breasts.

"I need to touch you," he'd whispered, and she'd needed him to do it, to taste her nipples, lick them, suck them into the heat of his mouth.

But she'd pulled back. She knew it had almost killed him, but he had let her do it.

"I can wait until you're ready, sweetheart," he'd whispered, and he'd drawn her against his hard body and held her in his arms through the long night.

Once, he'd asked why there were times he could see the sorrow of the world in her eyes.

Because everything you think you know about me is a lie.

She told herself she hadn't deliberately lied. He knew only what everyone else knew. That she was a student named Annie Stanton.

Then she and Declan grew close. Closer. And still she lied to him. Out of fear.

Not of him.

Never of him.

What she feared were the possible repercussions if he learned her true identity.

He was a warrior in the service of his country.

She was a princess of a kingdom that, because of her uncle, now had an uncertain relationship with the United States.

Could she ask Declan not to reveal her secret to his commanding officer? No. That would be asking him to dishonor his oath of loyalty. And if he told his commanding officer about her, what would happen next? Would his CO see too much risk in the situation? What if those further up the chain of command saw the diplomatic repercussions as impossible?

What if Declan ended up having to choose between her and the life he so clearly loved?

She'd decided she had to keep quiet==but keeping quiet was a polite way of saying she had to keep lying and eventually she'd known she couldn't go on doing it. For his sake and hers, she'd admitted that she had to end their relationship—but it was hard.

By then, she was deeply in love with him. Losing him would be agony. So she did it slowly.

She saw him less often.

She only took some of his calls.

She told him she was busy when she wasn't.

His growing bewilderment was painful. What had he done wrong? he'd asked. Had he somehow hurt her?

After a while, she felt as if her heart was breaking.

She'd decided to tell him everything. If he hated her for not telling him the truth sooner, she would live with it. If he had to stop seeing her, she would live with that too. She just couldn't inflict pain on him anymore.

In the end, Fate had the last laugh.

The same night she'd made that decision, she'd been jolted awake by the pressure of a hand over her mouth and another around her throat.

She'd tried to scream, but she couldn't. So she'd struggled instead, bucking and kicking and flailing her arms.

Her efforts had been useless, especially when a second pair of hands pinned her to the bed.

"Stop fighting," a low male voice hissed, "or I will apply enough pressure so that you lose consciousness."

"We do not wish to kill you unless we must, Princess Anoushka" a second voice said.

After a minute, the hand lifted from her throat.

"What do you want with me?" she'd gasped.

They told her that she had a choice. She could return to Qaram without protest—or return in a coffin.

Annie hadn't hesitated. "I will not return to Qaram. You'll have to kill me."

It had been a desperate bluff. Obviously, her uncle was determined to have her returned to his control.

That meant she was important to his plans. Surely, he would not want her dead.

And she was right—but in the worst possible way.

"Perhaps the princess requires a better incentive," one of them had said to his companion. Then he'd turned his cold eyes on her. "Here is a choice you may find more interesting, Princess Anoushka. You will return to your country with us—or your friend dies."

"My friend?" she'd said, even though she knew right away, she knew...

"Declan Sanchez," the second man said. "How does it feel to hold a man's life in your hands?"

Annie's thoughts had whirled. Declan was a skilled warrior—but these men were cold-blooded assassins. They would attack Declan when he was most vulnerable: when he was in his own home, asleep.

"Choose, Anoushka. And choose wisely."

She had begged to be permitted to leave a note. "People will wonder what happened to me."

The two men had exchanged knowing looks.

"They will be told you moved," the one who'd awakened her said. "Nothing of you will remain in these rooms."

"My landlord—"

"Your landlord just inherited a handsome sum of money. He is a happy man."

They gave her five minutes to get ready. An hour later, she'd been on a plane bound for Qaram.

The next time she saw Declan was at her friend's wedding in Texas.

At first, she'd been amazed her uncle Cyrus would

permit her to attend, but he'd said it was important to show a civilized face to the world.

And just in case she thought she could use the Texas visit to her advantage...He'd used the threat that always worked. Did she want Declan Sanchez to live—or to die?

"You won't be able to harm him," she said. "He'll be surrounded by his friends."

"His friends will not be able to save him," her uncle had said with an icy smile, "but in doing so, they will created an international incident. Imagine the headlines. *American Special Forces Solders Attack Qarami Diplomats at Texas Social Event.* Excellent, don't you think?"

Annie knew there would be no Qarami diplomats . There would only be her uncle's thugs, men whose job it was to keep her from running away, but she also knew that her uncle could, and would, spin the story to suit himself and effectively end Dec's career, if not his life.

The day of the wedding, her first view of Declan had damn near undone her.

She'd come dangerously close to throwing herself into his arms.

But she hadn't

Still, for the couple of minutes they were alone, she'd almost told him the truth.

And then sanity had returned.

Flying home, she'd told herself she'd survived the worst her uncle could do to her.

Wrong.

A few weeks later, he'd summoned her to his chambers and told her that she was about to do something of vital importance for her country.

"You will marry the king of Tharsalonia," he'd said.

She hadn't believed him. It had to be a threat meant to keep her in line. But it had not been a threat; it had been a fact.

Running away had not been an option. Her uncle had placed her under guard.

"For your own protection, Anoushka," he'd said, so earnestly that anyone who didn't know the truth would have believed him.

She'd even resorted to pleading—until she saw what pleasure that gave him. He had stolen her freedom. Her future. All she had left was her pride. She was determined to keep it, so she'd stopped pleading, stopped showing him any emotion at all. She refused to talk to him or join him at the functions he organized. Instead, she'd kept to her rooms and to the palace gardens.

"You need taming,," her uncle had said with grudging admiration. "The Tharsalonian king will enjoy your spirit."

But she'd refused to think about the Tharsalonian king until two days ago, when she'd been told she was being escorted to him...

Bang!

The door to the shed flew open.

Heart pounding, Annie struggled to her feet as two of her captors stormed into the room.

The ambassador's wife whimpered and cowered in

the corner. One of the men laughed, pointed his fingers at her and mimicked pulling a trigger.

The other man came for Annie, unshackled her, grabbed her by the arms and dragged her through the shed. When she stumbled, one of them kicked her in her backside and propelled her out the door.

At first, it was hard to get her bearings. She was dizzy. Disoriented. And the sun, setting over the jagged mountain peaks to the west, was in her eyes.

Sun or no sun, she was freezing. He teeth chattered, which seemed to amuse everybody. Every instinct she possessed warned her to show no weakness. So she took a deep breath and concentrated on maintaining self-control.

Gradually, her vision cleared. She looked about her. If by some miracle she had a chance to escape later tonight, when her captors had drunk themselves into a stupor, she'd have a mental map of the place.

The camp was in a grassy meadow. The bandits' vehicles—falling-apart Toyotas and a couple of ancient American trucks—were parked to one side. Smoke from half a dozen cooking fires rose into the sky.

Heavily armed men—Annie upped her initial estimate to thirty or more—in small groups. They had bearded faces, filthy hands and clothes. They were laughing and passing bottles of a colorless liquid that was probably vodka from hand to hand.

Clearly, some kind of celebration was underway.

Three men stood ahead of her under the branches of a tall pine. The man in the center was enormous, well over six feet tall and weighing at least three hundred pounds. From his bearing, she knew he was leader. Her fate surely lay in his hands. He was looking straight at her. She knew she was expected to look down and show submission.

The hell with that.

She kept her head up and her eyes on him. Seconds dragged by. Then he motioned her forward.

Her chin went up.

He folded his arms over his massive chest and said something. The men who'd taken her from the shack laughed. Her heart pounded, but she kept her face blank. No way was she going to show how frightened she was, and neither was she going to jump and obey commands.

The bandit who'd kicked her jabbed her with his rifle. She staggered forward. That sent everyone into paroxysms of laughter.

Annie's eyes narrowed. Without thinking, she swung around and glared at the man who'd poked her with the rifle.

"Put down that rifle and let's see just how brave you are!"

Did anyone know what she'd said? They certainly understood her tone of voice. It drew a long "oooh" from the crowd, as well as more laughter. She spun on her heel, drew her tattered silk gown as close around herself as she could, and strode towards the fat man.

"Princess," a voice whispered.

She shot a quick glance to the side and saw the American ambassador, hands tied, face bloodied and bruised.

"My wife?"

She hesitated, but only for a second. "Your wife is fine."

The ambassador shut his eyes, then opened them again. "Don't fight them," he said softly.

Annie kept walking. She saw a pile of crimson-colored rags with black polka dots out of the corner of her eye.

Ah, God!

It was a pile of bodies in a sea of blood, dotted with huge black flies.

She tried not to react, but it was impossible. She gagged, and that turned out to be a true knee-slapper. The bandits—the barbarians, she thought grimly—howled with laughter. So did their fat leader.

Annie took a long, steadying breath. *Don't,* she told herself *Don't get sick, not with them watching.*

It was hard, but she dragged her gaze from the bodies, forced down a mouthful of bile, and kept going.

When she was a couple of feet from the fat man, she stopped.

"Who are you?" she said in English. "Identify yourself immediately."

Okay. Maybe they all spoke English because there was a gasp behind her. The men on either side of him went stone-faced and reached into their robes.

This is it, Annie thought. *They're going to kill me.*

But, to her astonishment, Fat Man laughed. The men standing with him dutifully followed suit. *Ha ha,* they said, *ha ha.*

"You are either very brave or very foolish," the fat man said.

Annie drew herself up. "Do you know who I am?"

Another knee-slapper. Maybe she had a future in stand-up comedy—assuming she had a future at all.

"I am," she said, "the Princess Anoushka of the Royal House of Qaram."

Not even a blink.

"Do you know the power of the Royal House of Qaram?" she said. "You will be hanged for this insult unless you set me free."

"Why would I set you free when you are worth two millions American dollars to us?"

It was Fat Man doing a comedy routine now. Her uncle would never pay that kind of money for her.

"Qaram will not pay you. It will destroy you. You have a band of useless fighters. Qaram has an army. It has planes..."

Fat Man stepped forward and grabbed her arm. His thick fingers dug deep into her flesh. His stench was overwhelming and she tried to turn her face away, but he clasped her chin and forced her to look at him.

"Qaram is weak. So is Tharsalonia." He smiled, revealing yellowed teeth. "And neither will fight to get you back, not when they know who has claimed you."

Claimed? Why did the word made Annie's pulse skitter?

"You were on your way to be claimed today," the fat man said. "By the Tharsalonian king. How disappointed you must have been to learn that you were not going to be a bride." He leaned closer. Annie tried not to inhale. "But there is no need for disappointment, Princess. You will not be be married to the bridegroom you expected, but you will be married. Does that please you?"

Annie felt her courage falter, but she knew better than to let that show.

"You speak in riddles," she said.

Fat Man snapped his fingers. One of his men handed him a framed photograph. He shoved it into her hands.

"Look," he commanded.

She stared at the photo of a bearded man in his thirties or forties. His arms were folded over his chest, and he held a long, curved knife in one hand. The blade dripped with something dark.

But it was his eyes that were the focal point of the picture. They blazed with what could only be defined as insanity.

"Altair Amjad," Fat Man said. "Our Gift from Heaven, the Deliverer of Our People.'

Annie could almost hear the caps. And she knew the name. Amjad was said to have killed, tortured, raped and mutilated hundreds of people in these mountains.

She looked up from the photo. Fat Man's eyes burned with the same flame as Amjad's.

"He has need of a new wife."

Annie felt her heart kick into her throat.

"One who is fair of face and of royal blood. One who has been taught to be obedient." Another smile. "Although the Deliverer has told me that he is willing to teach her obedience himself—if she suits him in all other ways."

"No," Annie whispered. She wanted to sound strong, but her voice shook. "Absolutely not. Qaram will never allow—"

Fat Man drew back his hand and slapped her across the face. The blow was hard, and she staggered under the force of it.

"Chain her," he snarled. "If she makes any protest, beat her. We have the blessing of the Deliverer. He says if she shows signs of disobedience, her training may begin now." He flashed a yellow grin. "Just avoid her tits. He wants those for his own special training."

Everyone guffawed.

The same two men who'd taken her from the shed dragged her back to it.

Annie was stunned. No wonder her captors were celebrating. Two million dollars to turn her over to a man who would make the King of Tharsalonia look like a Boy Scout. More than ever, she had to find a way to escape

The two bandits shoved her through the shed door and cuffed to the wooden post again.

One of them stuck his hand between her legs. She gasped when he pinched her.

"Pleasant dreams, princess."

She held out until the door swung shut after them. Then she sank slowly to the floor.

Gingerly, she touched her cheek. It hurt, but the damage was negligible. What wasn't negligible was this nightmare.

It would go on and on and only get worse unless she came up with with something.

The ambassador's wife lay in the same fetal position, breathing hard and fast. Annie leaned towards her.

"Mrs. Carson?" she whispered. "I've seen your husband. He's fine."

No response, just the same rapid breaths.

"He said to tell you that he loves you."

Nothing. The woman was probably in shock.

"Mrs. Carson, " Annie said, striving to sound as matter-of-fact as possible, "we should try to get away. But I can't move." She shook her hand so the steel cuffs rattled. "Do you have a hairpin? A straight pin? Anything sharp." She waited, but there was no response. "You know what, Mrs. Carson? I bet that rope's long enough so you can get to the door. Wait awhile, give the bandits time to fall asleep. Then you could move to the door, peek out, see if there's a guard outside. Maybe he'll fall asleep and maybe you could reach his gun..."

And maybe pigs could fly.

Annie slumped back against the wall.

The ambassador's wife couldn't help anybody. And even if she had a pin, what good would it do? In the movies, people opened locks with pins, but this wasn't a movie, it was real life.

Annie had never felt more alone.

No.

That wasn't true.

She'd felt not just alone but abandoned after her

parents had died. Living in California under an assumed name, terrified each time someone looked at her a fraction of a second too long.

Then Declan Sanchez had come into her life, and everything had changed.

A sob rose in her throat. She choked it back, but not for long. Tears filled her eyes; she turned her head, buried her face against her shoulder and cried for all she had lost. Her parents. Her freedom. And Declan, the man she would never forget, the man she had fallen in love with.

The man who surely despised her.

At last, overcome by exhaustion, Annie fell into a dreamless sleep—

And woke to a man's big hand clamped over her mouth and the face of a monster staring down at her through four huge, bottomless eyes.

4

A scream bubbled from her throat, but the monster's hand forced it back.

If she couldn't scream, she could still fight. Kick. Flail. Twist.

"Stop it!"

Despite everything, she almost laughed. Stop? *Stop?* One of them was crazy and it wasn't she.

"Princess. Listen to me."

Annie grunted, jerked her chin down and sank her teeth into the creature's hand.

"Fuck," the thing growled, shoving her flat on her back and straddling her. "Dammit, you want to get both of us killed?"

If that was what it took to get this thing off her, yes. She wasn't the compliant creature her uncle and Fat Man wanted her to be. Her parents had raised to be strong and courageous, and if that meant fighting until there was no life left in her...

"Dammit, Annie, it's me!"

He felt her go still. An eternity seemed to pass. Then he felt the whisper of her breath against his palm. She was saying something. He couldn't really hear it...

Had she spoken his name?

There was only one way to be sure she knew it was him. The darkness. Her captivity. The four-eyed night goggles...

Dec yanked at the straps. The helmet came off and fell to the floor.

"Night goggles," he whispered. "See? It's me. Declan."

The woman he'd known as Annie stared up at him.

Thanks to a sliver of pale moonlight that had worked its way through a crack in the wall, he could see her face. She wasn't convinced. Well, why she be? She was handcuffed to a post; she'd endured hours of terror. She'd been dragged before the pig who led this bunch of outlaws and humiliated. Slapped in the face...

Dec felt a muscle knot in his jaw. He and the rest of his unit had seen it all from their observation point in the hills above the camp.

He'd almost gone crazy over that slap.

Chay had grabbed Dec's shoulder.

"You'll get her killed," he'd said, and after a long minute Dec had nodded, let out his breath, and settled back to wait.

There was a plan to get her out. All he had to do was follow it. They'd get the ambassador, his wife, and maybe the body of the embassy dude, but liberating Annie was the primary mission.

Correction. Liberating Princess Anoushka.

Right now, she was staring at him as if she'd never seen him before.

Dec leaned over her until they were a breath apart.

"It's me. Declan. You got that?"

She hesitated. Then she gave a quick nod.

"I'm going to take my hand away from your mouth. If you yell, if you do anything at all except stay quiet, we're gonna have a problem. Understand?"

Another quick nod.

Okay. She got it. She knew who he was...

Dammit.

She was crying. Well, so what? He didn't give a crap. It was just that he needed her trusting him, having no doubts about him.

He stroked his hand over her face, relearning the once-familiar feel of her. The high cheekbones, straight nose, delicately curved lips.

She shrank back.

Meaning, he thought grimly, she still wasn't entirely convinced.

"Hell," he murmured, and in that horrible place that stunk of fear and despair, he knew there was one fast way to convince the woman beneath him that he was real.

"Annie," he said, and he lowered his head and captured her mouth with his.

She tasted exactly as she always had. Sweet. Delicate. Perfect.

But how could he remember her taste? He'd put all of that aside...

Liar.

Everything in him remembered.

Not just her taste. More than that. The feel of her mouth under his. The softness of her body. The scent of her skin.

"Declan," she whispered. She pressed her hands against his chest. "Declan," she whispered again, and the way she said his name made him groan, draw her closer, closer...

What the fuck was he doing?

This woman wasn't his Annie. She was Qarami royalty, and he was here to get her out of the hands of the bandits who'd stolen her from her bridegroom.

Disgust for her, for himself, flooded his veins. He clasped her shoulders and pulled back.

"Convinced?" he said, amazed at how calm he sounded. "It's me. In the flesh. And if we don't get out of here fast, we might not get out at all. Can you stand?"

It took her a few seconds, but finally she nodded.

"Yes. But I'm handcuffed to this post."

Dec dug into his pocket. "Not a problem. I saw the cuffs when they brought you out a couple of hours ago."

"You mean, you've been watching?"

"Yeah. Just waiting for the right time. Hold your hand steady. Like that."

She leaned forward as he worked. Her hair brushed his face. There were burrs caught in the strands but the strands that swung free were silky and soft.

"Is that a hairpin?"

"It's pick. Comes down to almost the same thing."

The lock gave way, and Annie pulled free of the cuff. "Thank you."

"Is your wrist raw?"

"A little. Nothing to worry about. Declan? They have the American ambassador. And his wife. She's right here in this shed."

"She's already out. One of my guys has her."

"Is she okay?"

"She will be."

"There was another American. Someone from the embassy…"

"He's gone."

"Oh God! These horrible men—"

"You can be as upset as you want later. Right now, your job is to do as I say. You understand me, Princess?"

"Don't call me that."

"That's who you are."

"I'm not. I'm Annie."

"You're the Princess Anoushka," Dec said coldly. He took her hand and drew her to her feet, yanked off his jacket and wrapped it around her. "And I'm here to get back to your boyfriend, safe and sound."

"My what?"

"Your fiancé. The Tharsalonian king."

"Declan. Whatever you think you know—"

"Can you walk?"

"Will you listen? He is not—"

"You want to argue? Or you want to get the fuck out of here?"

She started to respond. Then she nodded.

"Okay," Dec said. "How do you feel?"

"I feel fine."

"I know you're probably a little weak—"

"I am never weak!"

Jesus, she'd almost snapped his head off. Dec wanted to laugh—but he didn't. Instead, he handed her a water bag. Her hands shook and he covered them with his and lifted the bag to her mouth.

"Not too much," he warned. "This is no time to get sick."

She nodded, slowed down, then let him take the water bag from her.

"What I meant about you feeling a little weak was that I'm sure you haven't had much to eat or to drink, and you've been chained up here for hours." He paused. "Unless I'm wrong and these gentlemen fed you steak and champagne before whirling you onto the dance floor."

It was a pathetic attempt at humor, but it worked. At least, it at won him a grudging smile. He needed more than that. He needed her full cooperation.

"I guess I do feel a little, you know, under the weather."

"The thing is, you're gonna have to dig down and work past that. I can't carry you out of this pigpen—I need my hands free in case we run into problems."

Annie nodded again. The shock of seeing him had

muddled her brain. What he meant by *problems* were the bandits outside.

"We've already neutralized several of them."

Neutralized. Despite herself, she winced.

"This isn't a Sunday School picnic," he said flatly. I suspect you've figured that out all by yourself."

"Yes. You're right. It's just that I never expected—"

"People hardly ever do."

"What about the ones who haven't been...neutralized?"

"They're drunk as skunks and snoring—but there's no guarantee the whole fucking camp won't suddenly decide it's wake-up time. So we're going to have to be quiet. No talking once we get through that door. You got that?"

"Yes."

"Okay. Time to move. Are you ready?"

She took a deep breath. "Yes."

He helped her to her feet. She swayed a little; he wrapped his arm around her waist.

"I'm going to go as quickly as I can," he said. "You'll have trouble keeping up."

"That's ridiculous. I'm every bit as capable as—"

"Didn't we just have this conversation?"

Annie rolled her eyes. He took that as a yes.

"So what I want you to do is lean into me. Not just on me. Into me. Let me take most of your weight. Understand?"

"Yes."

"Good. And one last thing." Dec cleared his throat. "If I go down—"

"No!"

He put his index finger across her lips.

"Believe me," he said, "I'm not planning on it. But if something happens, you're to keep going. Head for that big pine. The one where that fat SOB held court a few hours ago. There's a narrow trail just beyond it. It's steep, but you won't have to go far until one of the guys from the unit steps out and gets hold of you."

She lifted her face to his. Her eyes were wide; her mouth trembled.

"Declan. I couldn't stand it if you—if something happened to—"

He kissed her.

What the fuck. It had worked before. Kissing established him as being in charge. Or maybe it just reminded her of who he was. Of what they'd once had. What he'd thought they'd once had.

The point was, kissing her shut her up.

There was no other reason to kiss her.

Absolutely none.

THE MOON WORE a frothy veil of high white clouds. One second, pale ivory light illuminated the meadow. The next, the world was almost completely dark.

Walking without stumbling over something—a burned-out cook fire, a sleeping outlaw, a dead one—his guys had done their job well—would have been tough if Dec hadn't had the goggles on again.

And they damn well made the difference when a

figure clutching a long, wicked-looking blade loomed up ahead of them.

In one quick motion, Dec shoved Annie behind him, pulled his SOG-TAC knife from its scabbard, slipped it between his would-be assailant's ribs and angled the blade straight up into the prick's heart.

The bandit went down like a stone.

Dec heard the shocked intake of Annie's breath. He grabbed her hand and pulled her to him. She was trembling.

"Breathe," he whispered. "Breathe, dammit!" A second passed before he heard air shudder in and out of her lungs. "We have to keep moving. Okay?"

She gave a jerky nod. "Okay."

Yeah. Right. She was okay. That was why her teeth were banging together. Unfortunately, there was no time for niceties. He needed her to keep going. Who knew how long these pigs would take to sleep off the booze he'd watched them swill?

The good news was that he and the rest of STUD One had taken out some of them.

The bad news was that there were still lots of them left.

And getting clear of the encampment was only Part One of what it would take to get them to the extraction site. They had a lot of territory to cover, and it was anybody's guess if their escape route would be picked up or not.

But Annie was strong, just as she'd said. She followed his order to lean into him, matching his steps as best she could, and she didn't make a sound the couple of times he simply wrapped his arm even more tightly around her and lifted her off her feet so they could go faster.

Somebody coughed just a few feet away.

Dec froze.

Annie—dammit, Anoushka! He had to get that straight in his head. Anoushka froze, too. She burrowed into him. He could feel the race of her heart, hear the soft rush of her breath. He knew that she was terrified.

He wanted to gather her in, stroke her hair, put his mouth to hers. He wanted to tell her that he would never let anything happen to her no matter what it took...

She shuddered and buried her face against his shoulder.

It was crazy, but standing with her like this, holding her, the dangers around them seemed to slip away. For a handful of seconds, Dec was in another place. He was back in California, watching the sun set over the ocean with Annie in his arms.

He had never been happier.

And she—she had been playing games.

He'd seen a documentary one time about the Amish. Some of the Amish teenagers left their real lives for a year to try a modern kind of existence. Same with kids headed for college who took what they called a gap year and did the same thing. Have fun, forget what lay ahead, just get out there and do something totally different.

He had been Annie's something totally different. Her walk on the wild side.

But not wild enough to include sex.

He'd attributed it to a sweet, old-fashioned modesty, but he knew better now.

Where she came from, a woman hung onto her virginity because sex had nothing to do with desire and everything to do with her value as a bride. And now here he was, the guy who'd helped her keep her virginity, about to deliver her to the guy who'd bought it.

Somewhere, he though bitterly, the gods had to be laughing.

The coughing that had stopped their forward progress had turned into snoring.

It was safe to start walking again.

They reached the outer perimeter of the encampment and passed the big pine tree. The land began to rise. They were on a narrow, tree-lined trail that grew steeper and steeper. Walking two abreast became impossible. Annie fell in behind Dec; he hung onto her hand and helped her scramble uphill.

The trail widened again when they reached a tangle of brush. Dec stopped so abruptly that she walked into him.

He put a finger to his lips.

A minute went by. Two minutes. They were surrounded by silence. Then it was broken by the faint whistle of a night bird.

Except it wasn't a bird.

It was Chay Olivieri, armed to the teeth, stepping into their path.

"Good to see you, dude. We were starting to think you'd decided you liked the company down there so much you were gonna hang around for a while."

Dec grinned. "You know how it is, man. Nobody wants to be the first to leave a party." His grin faded. "The ambassador? His wife?"

"Got 'em both."

Chay turned and they climbed another quarter mile until they reached a small clearing. The ambassador and his wife stepped forward. The wife was pale and silent, but the ambassador was smiling.

"Thank you, Lieutenant Sanchez. Our thanks to all of you."

Dec nodded and turned to Chay "Everybody got back okay?"

The men of STUD One stepped forward. Annie laughed and opened her arms.

"Nick! Chay! Alex! Danny! Aidan! I am so happy to see you guys!"

"Hey, Annie." Aidan reached out to hug her.

Dec stopped him.

"Save the celebration for the extraction site," he said sharply. "Right now, we're wasting time. We left lots of calling cards down there. First light'll be in a couple of hours and somebody's sure to wake up and notice. Plus we have a three hour hike ahead of us." He eyeballed each man individually. "And let's remember who we have here. The lady's name isn't Annie. She's Princess Anoushka."

"No," Annie said quickly. "Really, I'm just—I'm just me."

Dec bent down and scooped his pack from where he'd left it.

"You're just you. The Princess of Qaram. Isn't that what I said?" He dug in the pack, took out a stack of camo stuff: sweater, pants, jacket, heavy socks, plus a pair of combat boots. "The smallest sizes I could come up with," he said, tossing the stuff to her. "Get it on, fast."

Nick cleared his throat. "Dec," he said softly, "maybe she needs a minute..."

"We don't have a minute." He knew how he sounded. Gruff. Cold. Well, this wasn't a Sunday hike in the country. And she wasn't going to get any special treatment, not from him. "Go on," he snapped. "Get that stuff on."

Annie didn't argue. She simply stepped behind a shrub and emerged a couple of minutes later dressed in what he'd given her, carrying his jacket and what remained of her gown. He took them from her, put on the jacket, dumped the gown in his pack and came up with an energy bar and a water bag.

"Not fit for royalty," he said, "but it's the best we've got."

His men were all staring at him. Too bad. If they thought he sounded like he had a ramrod up his ass, fuck 'em.

He had a job to do and he was doing it.

"Okay," he said briskly. "Olivieri, you take point.

Maguire, you're second. Mr. Ambassador, you're next, and after you, your wife."

"My wife can walk with me," the ambassador said. "Isn't that right, dear?"

Dec decided not to argue. He'd prefer them all in single file—it would be a little harder to take them out that way—but the woman looked as if she'd never make it on her own.

"Fine. Sullivan, you're behind the ambassador and his wife. Princess, you're in back of Sullivan. Spanos, you're next. Then Romano. I'll take up the rear. Clear?"

They all nodded. STUD One shrugged on their packs and shouldered their weapons.

The moon had finally broken free of the clouds, which meant there was no longer a need for night goggles.

"I'm figuring an hour to reach the ridgeline, then a five minute break. No stopping for anything after that. We have to make the extraction point by oh six hundred. So let's go."

The break would be for the civilians. The Unit could keep going for hours, even on this terrain, a narrow, rocky game trail through increasingly dense forest.

There was an easier route and Dec hoped the bandits would assume that was the one they'd chosen. Add in that the camp probably wouldn't stir for another hour or even two, top that off with Maguire and Romano having disabled as many of the bandits' vehicles as they could, and STUD One and its rescued hostages had a good head start.

The fly in the ointment was not knowing how quickly the bandits would communicate with the others who'd want to find them—Annie's uncle, the Tharsalonians, Altair Amjad. Almost anybody could be coming after them, but Dec could only operate on what he knew.

So, yeah, this climb was safer.

It was also a hell of a lot rougher.

Ten minutes in, the ambassador's wife dropped to her knees. Her husband got her on her feet and put his arm around her. Alex Spanos stepped up on her other side and draped her arm around his neck.

"Easy," Mrs. Carson," he said gently. "We've got you."

Dec's job as last man was to check what might be happening behind them. So far, so good. There was no sign of anybody, no sounds carrying to them on the still air.

They were making decent time.

Annie was still going strong.

He watched her as she struggled up a particularly steep stretch of ground. Sullivan looked back and offered her his hand, but she waved it away.

Dec wasn't really surprised. He knew she was strong. And courageous. One day in California, she'd asked him if he know how to surf and when he'd said yeah, he did, her eyes had lit up.

"Will you teach me?" she'd asked.

He'd been hesitant. She was small. Delicate. And the waves on the beach he surfed were sometimes towering. But she'd been persistent and finally he'd taken her out with him, showed her the basics on a board he'd borrowed for her—and damn if she hadn't gotten the hang of it quickly enough to ride a couple of good-size waves, laughing with joy as she did, not complaining or even showing fear the times she got dumped.

Afterwards, back at his place, she'd gone into the bathroom to shower. She'd emerged wearing his terrycloth robe. He'd laughed when he saw her. He was six feet two to her, what, five feet four. The robe had been like a tent on her, hanging to her feet, the sleeves rolled up, the sheer size of it swallowing up her sweet curves.

"What?" she'd said, with mock indignation, and he'd grabbed the lapels of the robe and tugged her into his arms, and she'd laughed with him until their eyes met and, slowly, God, slowly he'd reached out, opened the robe and for the first time saw her, all of her, naked and rosy and so beautiful it had almost killed him not to touch her...

Dec shuddered.

They were at the ridgeline.

"Take five," he said, his voice hoarse.

The men, trained to making the most of every second of downtime, shrugged off their packs and sat wherever they could find a reasonably comfortable spot.

Dec dumped his pack as well and headed for the ambassador and his wife.

"You doing okay, sir?"

The ambassador was breathing hard, but he gave Dec a thumb's up.

"Been doing some running the last couple of years," he panted. "It's paying off."

It didn't take much to see that the guy's wife wasn't doing so well. She was wearing camos, same as Annie, but they only emphasized the woman's removal from reality. She sat with her hands folded in her lap and a faraway expression on her face.

"You're doing fine, ma'am," Dec said gently.

She flinched when he touched her shoulder. Dec drew his hand back and walked over to Maguire.

"Help the ambassador's wife when we move out," he said softly.

Aidan nodded. "Yeah. I figured on it."

Dec headed for the princess.

She was sitting on a flat rock, long legs stretched out in front of her. He handed her a water bag.

"Thanks," she said, and tilted her head back to drink.

Water trickled down her chin, down her throat.

He imagined bending to her, following that drop with his tongue, tasting the coolness of the water, the heat of her skin...

Jesus Christ.

He swung on his heel, strode past everybody to where he'd left his pack and dug through it until he found another water bag.

What he really needed to find was his composure.

A hard-on? Here? Really? With death behind them

and a two, three hour scramble up the mountain ahead of them?

Dec took a long drink of water. Then he got his stuff together and rose to his feet.

"Move it out," he barked.

The line formed up and they started forward again.

TWO HOURS and twenty minutes later, the land began to level off and the trees began to thin.

Dec called a halt and checked first his GPS and then his map—the old tried-and-true methods could be comforting.

They were five clicks from the extraction point. The sky had lightened to the color of pewter. There was still no sound or sign that they were being followed. All good stuff, although the absence of anybody coming after them made Dec uneasy.

He knew the other guys were uneasy too. It was hard to believe this could continue to go so smoothly.

"How much further?"

Dec swung towards the ambassador. He wasn't looking so good anymore. His face was a bright red and his hands trembled as he unwrapped an energy bar.

His wife looked even worse. Her skin was chalky. She still hadn't spoken. A thin line of saliva was visible at the corner of her mouth.

"Not far," Dec said. "Another forty, fifty minutes."

The ambassador nodded. "I don't think my wife can hold out much longer."

"Just a little bit more, sir, I promise."

"Declan?"

Dec turned around. The princess had come up behind him. She hadn't spoken to him since their last break.

"Declan." She ran the tip of her tongue over her bottom lip. "You said a helicopter will pick us up."

"Yes."

She nodded. "Where will it take us?"

Dec frowned. "I don't know."

"To your base in California?"

"A Black Hawk couldn't do that kind of distance."

"I know that. What I meant was, is that our final destination? The States?"

It was a good question, but he didn't have the answer. "It'll be someplace safe."

"Someplace safe," she whispered.

Something in her voice worried him. The look of her worried him too. She was pale. Damp with sweat. A lock of hair hung over her eye. Without thinking, he pushed it back.

"Why are you asking? Is there a place that wouldn't feel safe to you?"

"I just—I just—" She took a deep breath. "I'm just was wondering where we'll be going, that's all."

Of course she was wondering. Any bride whose wedding had been delayed would want assurance that she was going straight into the arms of her groom.

Dec's mouth twisted.

"Don't worry about a thing, Princess," he said with a cold smile. "I'm sure the United States government has no interest in depositing you anyplace but in your bridegroom's lap."

He swung away from her and shouldered his gear. He could feel her staring after him. His guys were watching him too. So what? Was he supposed to treat her as if she were special?

His job was to get her out.

If she didn't like the way he was dealing with her, fuck it.

Something cold and wet splatted against his forehead. He looked up and saw a sky that had filled with rainclouds. Shit. The forecast hadn't included rain, but weather was always unpredictable when you were up this high.

"Let's move," he said sharply.

The only good news was that they were on the last few miles of a journey he already wanted to forget.

THE RAIN TURNED into a steady downpour.

They stopped just long enough to put on ponchos. There weren't enough to go around so Alex and Nick gave theirs to the ambassador and his wife.

Aidan tried to give his to the princess, but she refused it.

"Thank you," she said, "but I'm fine," even though any idiot could see she was soaked and shivering

Dec watched for a few seconds. Then he cursed, strode over and pulled his own poncho over her head.

"Do us all a favor," he said. "Stop trying for the Mother Teresa award and just do as you're told."

She looked at him the way he figured she'd look at somebody who'd just kicked a puppy.

"I don't know why I ever thought I missed you," she said in a shaky whisper, and then she brushed past him and started along the trail, her pace so rapid that Maguire, who was the new point man, had to scramble to get out ahead of her.

The others trudged past Dec.

"The only award anybody's tryin' for here is Asshole of the Year," Romano muttered.

Dec chewed on that for a while, which was why it took him another couple of miles until he realized exactly what the princess had said.

That she'd missed him. Or that she'd thought she'd missed him.

A jolt of elation shot through his blood—until he thought about it.

No matter what she'd said, it didn't change the facts.

She'd left him. No note. No nothing. And the next time he saw her, at that wedding, all fancied up in silk and jewels, bodyguards watching out for her, a big chauffeured Mercedes waiting in the driveway, he'd understood the reason.

He had never been what she wanted.

Fine.

She'd never been what he wanted either.

She was a woman who would expect—what did they call it? Commitment. Well, he wasn't into commitment. He liked his life the way it was. He had the world's best job, a place on the beach, enough hot women to keep him busy 24/7.

Give that up?

Hell, no.

And, come to think of it, she wouldn't have wanted commitment. The woman he'd believed her to be would have wanted it, but she wasn't that woman. She was a princess, meaning she really never would have wanted a man like him at all...

"Dec?"

Dec looked up. Chay had fallen in alongside him.

"Yeah," Dec said, "okay, I know I'm being a little hard on her, but—"

"Something's not right," Chay said. "I can feel it."

Dec felt the hair rise on the back of his neck.

Chay was part Sioux. He was the best tracker in any of the units and he had what they all referred to as this sensing thing. He'd get a feeling—somebody was watching them, somebody was hiding up ahead. At first, they'd teased him about it. And he'd laughed and said things like yeah, if only he'd been on the plains with Custer...

But damned if he wasn't right seventy, eighty percent of the time. After a while, they'd all learned to take him seriously.

Dec gave him a sideward glance.

"You think they're behind us? I checked a few minutes ago and—"

"So did I. Nothing."

"Ahead of us, then," Dec said in a low voice.

"Yeah. Somebody's out there. And the closer we get to the extraction site, the more I feel it."

Dec nodded. They were on a plateau now. Soon, the land would open up, except for the forest pressing on on either side.

Just right for an ambush.

"Move up to the front of the line," he said. "Tell everybody to fall back."

Seconds later, STUD One and its three rescued hostages were gathered around him.

"Okay," Dec said quietly. "We're no more than ten minutes from where the Black Hawk will pick us up." He paused. "It's possible we're no longer alone."

The ambassador tightened his hold on his wife. "You mean, we're being followed?"

"I mean that these mountains are home to these bandits. They know every trail, every pass, every switchback. It's possible they went around us, that they're waiting for us somewhere ahead. They have to figure we're getting out by helicopter and there are only a couple of places where a bird could land, Maybe they guessed which we're using—and guessed right."

He looked at the faces of those grouped around him.

The men of STUD One looked resolute. They were tough, battle-hardened, and fighting their way out would not come as anything new.

The ambassador looked worn. His wife's expression was still a blank.

No surprises so far—until he got to Annie.

Her expression was not one of fear, it was of unwavering determination. Flattened mouth. Narrowed eyes. She looked like a woman who'd come to a conclusion...

But about what?

"Princess? You have something to say?"

She looked at him. Hesitated. Shook her head.

"Okay." Dec cleared his throat and focused his attention on the three hostages. "We're going to do these last few minutes as quickly as possible. We're also going to change formation. You three will stay together with us clustered around you." He checked his watch. "We should get to the extraction site just as the Black Hawk touches down. You'll run for it. Run, not walk. Mr. Ambassador, Lieutenant Olivieri will carry your wife. None of you are to turn back to check what's happening behind you. You'll make for the 'copter, grab the hands of those waiting to pull you on board, and that's it. Any questions?" Nobody spoke. Dec nodded. "Fine. In that case—"

"Lieutenant?"

"What is it, Princess?"

"Actually, I do have a question. It's the same one I asked before. Where will the helicopter take us?"

Dec's mouth thinned. "The big question for you, obviously."

"Do you know or don't you, Lieutenant? Where will they take us? Where will they take me?"

Lieutenant. Is that who he was to her? Yes. Damn right. He was Special Ops, and she was his mission.

"We're dealing with a COM blackout," he said brusquely. "A communications blackout for the next..."

Dec glanced at his watch. "...for the next eight minutes. Once I make contact, I'll ask."

The look on her face changed. It wasn't that she no longer looked resolute, it was only that she looked...different.

"Thank you, Lieutenant."

Dec flashed a cool smile. "Nothing to thank me for, Your Highness. We live to serve."

They moved out. The ambassador was doing his best, but his pace was flagging. His wife was stumbling along between Chay and Aidan.

The princess was still matching his men's pace.

Why not?

A bride wouldn't want to be late to her wedding.

At the six minute mark, Dec dug out his dug his satphone. He, Black and Andy Stein had agreed not to use it until the last minutes for fear of being tracked. Now, those last minutes were fast approaching.

Dec punched a button. The response, though marred by static, was immediate.

"Recovery One, what is your situation? Over."

"Recovery Base, we are five minutes out. Over."

"Recovery One, pickup coming in early. ETA four minutes."

Dec grunted. Assuming Olivieri was right and they were walking into a welcoming party, the sooner the better.

"We can be there in four, Recovery Base."

"Do so. We want to make this a quickie."

The Black Hawk would kiss the grass, they'd all scramble onboard, and the helicopter would take off.

"Understood, Recovery Base. Okay. Ove—"

An elbow dug into his ribs. The princess. They were moving fast, damn near running. She looked exhausted, and, despite the poncho, soaked from head to toe, but she hadn't forgotten what she'd asked him to find out.

Dec rolled his eyes. "Recovery Base. What is the drop-off location for our packages? I have been asked for an answer. Over."

There was a squawk of static. A pause. Then the COM guy was back.

"Recovery One. Mr. and Mrs. Dapper Dan will take a sea voyage."

Dec nodded. The ambassador and his wife would be landed on an aircraft carrier in the Persian Gulf.

"And the third package? Over?"

"Drop off point is the Q place. Home Sweet Home. Any more questions? Over."

"No more questions, Recovery Base. Over."

"Recovery One? Good luck."

Dec disconnected. Annie tugged on his sleeve.

"Where?" she gasped.

"Wait a second..." He narrowed his eyes, peered through the rain. Yes. There it was, dead ahead. An open stretch of meadow. And the whomp-whomp of a Black Hawk coming in, visible now against the rainy sky.

Five hundred yards.

Four hundred.

The Black Hawk was coming in fast.

"Okay," Dec yelled. "Move. Move. Move."

"Declan. Please. Tell me. Where will they take me?"

The woman was certifiable. They were running at top speed, darkly ominous woods all around them, and she was still worried about her destination?

"Qaram," he said, "Safe and sound."

She stumbled to a stop. "No!"

Dec grabbed her arm and hauled her along with him. "Jesus," he growled, "keep moving. What do you mean, no? You'll be a couple of days late for your wedding, sure, but—"

"Don't let them take me back to Qaram! Or to Tharsalonia! Please! I'm begging you, Declan. I can't go back. I won't go back. I—"

The world exploded.

Gunfire spat from the woods to the east.

The men of STUD One spun in that direction and began returning fire. Sullivan and Spanos lobbed grenades. Screams and the roar of small arms fire and explosives filled the air.

"Go," Dec shouted. "Go. Go. Go. Get the hostages out of here. Go!"

Romano grabbed the ambassador by the arm and raced for the helicopter. Olivieri tossed the ambassador's wife over his shoulder and did the same. Sullivan, Spanos and Maguire ran backwards so they could provide covering fire.

"Run," Dec yelled at Annie as he fired into the trees.

She didn't move.

"Annie! Did you hear me? Run!"

She shook her head. "I'm not going back."

She wasn't going back? What in hell? Was she crazy?

Maybe the world had gone crazy, because even as he tried to process that, a horseman, fuck, a *horseman* came galloping out of the woods

DEC TOOK AIM, shot the guy out of his saddle and spun Annie in the direction of the Black Hawk.

"Move," he roared. "Goddammit, woman—"

"I'll be a prisoner again."

"What?"

"My uncle sold me to the king of Tharsalonia. I won't go back, Declan! I'd sooner die here than go back."

Jesus Christ, what in hell was she talking about?

Maybe he hadn't heard her right. Between the whomp-whomp of the rotors, the roar of Kalishnikovs and the bark of HK MP7s...

But, yes, he must have heard her right, because she was refusing to move, turning them both into easy targets for the rounds of hot ammo flying around them. That they hadn't been hit already was some kind of miracle.

"Sanchez!"

The shout came from the helicopter. Romano was leaning out the open door, gesturing, yelling, urging Dec and Annie to run to the bird.

"I can't go back, "Annie sobbed. "Please. Just leave me here. Leave me. Save yourself, Declan, but leave me!"

The Black Hawk was starting to rise.

They were almost out of time.

Dec knew that in the seconds that were left, he could grab Annie, dump her over his shoulder, race for the 'copter and figure out what to do with her later.

Except, there would be no later.

Their first stop would be the closest one.

Qaram.

Another rider was thundering towards them. Dec fired. The guy tumbled from his saddle. The horse, reins dangling, kept coming.

"Son of a bitch!" Dec snarled.

He stepped into the path of the terrified horse. It shied away, but he grabbed for the reins, snagged them and swung into the saddle.

"Annie!"

He yelled her name, leaned over, his arm extended towards her. She grabbed his hand. He hoisted her up behind him.

The last thing he saw as they galloped for the trees was the Black Hawk gaining altitude as it rose over the meadow.

5

They made it into the forest.

The trees were tall, their trunks massive. There wasn't lots of space between them. Moving as fast as they were that could have been a problem, but the horse seemed to know the place and threaded his way through without any encouragement.

That was good.

Even better was the amount of fire the Black Hawk was putting down.

Dec knew that it couldn't stay on the scene much longer and there was no way of knowing how many men were in pursuit, but the helicopter would take out a lot of them out.

He hoped.

The horse was big, fast and smart. It gave Dec all the speed he asked, but he knew there was a limit to how long and how far he could make such demands of the animal before it faltered.

You didn't grow up on the Nebraska plains without knowing something about horses.

Annie's arms were wrapped around his waist. She was leaning into him. He had the feeling she knew horses, too, and that was a damned good thing considering that they were all but flying.

"Ahead of us," Annie gasped in his ear. "Some kind of trail..."

Dec saw it. To their right, a narrow opening that wound down through the trees, probably into a valley.

To their left, the land rose higher and higher. There was no discernible trail.

The sounds of gunfire, of the helicopter, had faded. Dec risked a quick look over his shoulder. Nobody behind them...yet.

The trail leading downhill was coming up fast.

Taking it was the logical choice. Heading further up the mountain would be crazy. The climb was going to be rough. There was no trail. And there was no promise of what they'd find at the top.

But every instinct Dec possessed told him that logic had no place in what was rapidly becoming a puzzle as complex as any he'd ever experienced.

Dec slowed the horse. Took one last glance at the downhill trail.

Then he touched the horse's flanks lightly with his boot heels and turned the animal uphill.

~

THEY RODE FOR HOURS, the horse picking its way

between trees, its pace quickening when the trees thinned out and the land flattened, but then the land would rise again and the horse would slow.

The uphill portions were steep, plus the animal was carrying two riders.

The rain stopped.

That, at least, improved things.

They took a short break. Annie took off her poncho and shook it out. Dec put it back in his pack. They gulped down water—the horse drank from Dec's cupped hands—and then they got moving again.

They hadn't heard gunfire in a very long time. Still, Dec wanted to put as much distance as possible between them and whoever it was who'd attacked them back at the rendezvous point.

Who had turned into the million dollar question.

Was it the men who'd kidnapped her? That made sense, but the terrorists led by Altair Amjad were just as likely suspects. And what about the king she'd been on her way to marry, or her own uncle, the man she said had held her prisoner and sold her to the king?

And, really, now that he thought about it, what did it matter?

There were people who wanted to capture Annie and kill him, and no way was he going to let either thing happen. And, yeah, he was back to thinking of her as Annie. It didn't take a genius to know that she'd left her other identity in that clearing where the Black Hawk had landed and then lifted off without them on board.

Jesus, what a mess.

They were on unknown terrain with who knew how many enemies on their asses. And, man, he didn't want to think about what had to be going on back at Camp Condor. By now, Black would know what had gone down. He'd be running in circles trying to figure out why the fuck Dec had taken off with the woman he'd been charged with rescuing instead of getting her safely on that helicopter.

It was entirely possible that he'd go home to a court-martial. Assuming he managed to get home and right about now, the odds on that weren't looking so great.

The horse slowed its pace.

Dec let it.

Another hour passed. The horse stumbled, then recovered its footing, but Dec knew it couldn't go much further.

He drew back on the reins.

He felt Annie sit up straight behind him. Crazy, but even with everything around them going to shit, he hated losing the feel of her breasts and belly warm against his back.

"Are we stopping?"

He nodded. "We need to give this guy a break."

Annie swung her leg over the horse's rump and jumped lightly to the ground. Dec did the same., then patted the animal's glossy flank as it blew out a long breath.

"I know just how you feel, pal. It's been a rough day."

Annie peered through the trees. "How much further to the top?"

"Good question." Dec dumped his pack and his rifle against a tree, dug his binoculars out, hung them around his neck, reached for a low branch and climbed until he had a clear view of what lay ahead.

At first, all he saw was more forest. Then he began to see a change. The land flattened into what appeared to be a sea of grass and beyond it...

More mountain.

No road. No houses. Nothing—until a slow scan with the binoculars showed him a craggy outcropping of rock and what looked like a pond or maybe a swamp.

Excellent. A rock wall at their backs would offer some protection from the cold and from predators, including the human kind, and they'd have water to refill their bags. Aside from finding a village, it was more than he'd hoped for.

"Did you see anything?" Annie asked when he reached the ground.

"Our camp for the night."

He took water and energy bars from his pack. He had a couple of MREs but he figured on saving them for supper.

They each had some water, and he gave the horse another drink. Then they unwrapped the bars and bit into them.

"Mmm," Annie said.

Dec laughed. "I've heard people say lots of things about energy bars, but 'mmm' isn't one of them."

"No?"

"No."

"Well, maybe I lucked out." She took another bite. "For instance, this particular bar is—let's see. Vanilla with fudge."

"Vanilla with fudge, huh?"

"You mean," she said, with wide-eyed innocence, her "yours isn't?"

He knew damn well hers tasted exactly like his—a combination of oats, raisins, sticky stuff that approximated caramel, and little black dots that were either seeds or best left as a mystery.

"No way," he said solemnly. "Mine is strawberry."

"Of course."

"Of course?"

"Remember that little ice cream stand? The one up the beach? Each time we went there, you'd read through the list of flavors and then you'd say, "Well, I think I'll have strawberry...""

Her words died away. So did her smile and his.

"Declan," she said in a shaky whisper, "I'm so sorry. So terribly sorry."

Yeah. So was he.

For a minute there, he'd let his memories take over.

The long afternoons on the beach. Ice cream cones —vanilla fudge for her, strawberry for him—at a little place the tourists never seemed to find.

They'd found a lot of places like that, ones that were secrets known only to lovers.

A coffee shop that they'd decided made the best lattes in the world.

A tiny cove nobody ever visited except the two of them—and a pod of dolphins.

A hole-in-the-wall just outside town that served hot dogs with chili.

Hot dogs with chili? Annie had said the same way someone who'd never read *Alice in Wonderland* would say *A rabbit with a watch?*

Then she'd taken her first bite, rolled her eyes and said *Oh my god, Declan, I think I'm in love.*

She'd laughed and he'd laughed—and, fuck, what a bad thing to remember, because what he also remembered was that as he'd watched her dig into the hot dog he'd thought, *What about being in love with me?*

And all the time, all the goddamn time, she'd been living a lie so big he could hardly get his head around it, playing a game before she went back to her real life.

But he wouldn't mention it, wouldn't question it, wouldn't say a word...

"How could you have lied to me all those months?"

So much for not saying a word. Even worse, he sounded like a pimply-faced teenager whose girlfriend had tossed him aside for the high school quarterback.

Yeah. But it was too late to call back what he'd said. What the hell. He might as well go for it.

"Did you hear what I said, Annie? Why did you lie to me?"

That was better. Now he sounded the way he felt. Cold with anger, not numb with pain. This was not the time or place for this. The logical part of him knew that, but did she really think the *I'm sorry* she'd tossed at him a while ago was going to make him forget what she'd done?

"I never lied about us," she said, looking stricken. "About you and me."

"There was no you and me. Hell, forget that. There was a me. But it turns out there wasn't really a you."

"Declan. You have to believe me. I wanted to tell you…"

"I'm just a humble little orphan," he said, his tone a nasty, high-pitched parody of hers.

"I never said that! You asked about my family. I said my parents were dead. And that was the truth."

"Your parents." He grasped her shoulders. "Interesting that you never mentioned that daddy and mommy were the king and queen of Qaram."

"Declan." She twisted a little under his hands. "You're hurting me."

He probably was. He could feel his fingers digging into her flesh. So what? A little physical pain was nothing compared to what he'd felt all these weeks.

"And telling me you were Canadian. I suppose that was the truth too."

A flush rose in her cheeks. "You asked about my accent."

"Right. And you figured, hey, Canada's only, what, six, seven thousand miles from Qaram? That's close enough."

Tears glittered in her eyes. Did she think that would influence him? Because it wouldn't. Not anymore.

"I didn't want to lie to you!"

"Then why did you?"

"I couldn't—I couldn't tell you the truth. Not at the beginning, when we first met. And then, after we'd been together for a while—"

"We were never together," he said coldly. "You saw to that."

He could tell by the little furrow that appeared between her eyebrows that she didn't understand what he meant. The she got it, and the color in her face deepened.

"You meant..." Her voice trembled. "You meant everything to me."

"Yeah. I bet."

"You did! You were my best friend."

"Your best friend?" She gasped as he hoisted her to her toes. He was close to being out of control and he knew it, he knew it, but Christ, he'd had his fill of her lies, of her pretense to be some sweetly innocent young thing. She owed him the truth and it was about time she understood that he wasn't going to settle for anything less. "Is that what I was when you spent hours lying in my arms? When I kissed you and you moaned and opened your mouth to me? When I held you through those long nights when you wept and wouldn't tell me why?"

"It was wrong. I should have told you. I know that now, but you were—I just said, you were my best friend and—and—"

"Fuck being your best friend," he growled, and he bent his head and kissed her.

Not gently. Not tenderly. Not even with compassion

for what she'd endured the last few hours and days. He kissed her with pent-up fury at her for what she'd done to him, at himself for not seeing through her from the start...

And then he tasted salt on her lips and he knew she was crying, and he groaned, cupped her face with his hands and kissed her as he'd dreamed of kissing her all the endless weeks they'd been apart.

Her response was immediate, and everything he could have wanted.

She leaned into him, moaned, and gave herself up to his kiss.

It was the way she'd always responded to him, as if he were the only man she would ever want. It all came back, the memories, the joy and then the pain, the anguish of losing her, and he gathered her in his arms, and she put her hands on his chest, slid them to his shoulders...

The horse whinnied.

Dec froze.

He drew Annie's hands down.

She opened her eyes and stared at him.

"Be quiet," he said in a rasping whisper.

He could feel his heart pumping as he eased his pistol from its holster. Annie was staring at him, her eyes wide with fear. He motioned her to get down and when she didn't move fast enough, he put his hand on her shoulder and shoved her to the ground.

The horse, head up, ears cocked, nickered again.

Dec scanned the woods around them. Nothing moved or stirred. There were sounds, but they were those that belonged in a forest: the whisper of leaves shifting in the slight, the call of birds in the branches.

As far as he could tell, everything was the way it should have been.

A deer stepped from the trees ahead. The horse jerked his head up and down as if to say, *See? I told you there was something coming.*

Dec let out his breath, holstered the pistol, reached for Annie and brought her to her feet.

"Just a deer," he said briskly. "You good to walk?" She nodded and he dumped the wrappers from the energy bars into his pack, swung the pack over his shoulder and set off.

She fell in behind him.

"Declan?"

"Yeah?"

"What we were just talking about...."

"How about concentrating on keeping up with me? The sun won't be setting for a few more hours, but it'll be dark in these woods before that. Another half a mile—"

She stumbled. He swung around and steadied her.

"Declan? I only wanted to say—"

"Do us both a favor, princess. Just pay attention to where you put your feet."

She looked crestfallen. Had he hurt her feelings? So what? Her feelings didn't matter a damn. And what had just happened, that kiss, would not, could not happen again.

Keeping the two of them alive was what this was all about.

And, yes, he was still attracted to her, but attraction, the old male-female thing, was all it was.

It was true that he wanted to know why she'd lied to him, but it wasn't personal. Not anymore...

Except, instinct told him that the reason for the lie held the key to what was happening now. She was willing to risk everything rather than return to Qaram.

Why?

Yeah, there was her story. That her uncle had kept her prisoner. That he'd sold her to the king of Tharsalonia. It sounded like something out of a bad fairy tale.

Why would he believe it?

On the other hand, why spin such a story?

Never mind.

Right now, what mattered was finding a way out of this mess. Make camp for the night, then figure out how to get the princess to safety. And yes, he was back to thinking of her by her title. It had been a mistake to think of her any other way.

And whether he wanted to hear her story or not wasn't up for grabs. He had to hear it. Was she at risk, they way she claimed, or wasn't she? The truth would affect what he'd already done, what he did next, what he'd tell Recovery Base.

Once they got out of these woods and found shelter, he'd interrogate her.

Meanwhile, he needed to keep his attention on the forest, the mountain...

The horse.

The horse was flicking it ears. It was quickening its gait. Dec understood enough horse language to know that meant that something good was ahead. Food? Water?

Its rightful owner?

Why take chances? Maybe what the animal sensed was good for horses, but not so good for two people on the run.

He clucked softly to the horse and tugged on the reins. The animal blew out heavily and came to a stop.

Annie stumbled into him, then jerked back. "Sorry,"

Dec didn't bother answering. She was worn out. So was he. All of them—woman, man, horse—needed a rest.

He took his binoculars from his pack.

"What do you see?"

What he saw was salvation.

Another few hundred feet and they'd be out of the trees and in that grassy meadow he'd spotted during that last break.

The horse whinnied. It wanted to get to the paradise just ahead, but experience and training had taught Dec to be cautious.

He looked at the princess.

"We're going to reach open ground in a few minutes. When we do, you'll stay in the trees with the horse."

"Declan." She hesitated. "What I was telling you before—"

"Do you understand? You'll stay hidden until I signal."

"Yes. I understand—but—but I want you to know

that—that what I said about you being my best friend was—"

"It was bullshit." He saw her face whiten. Too bad. "There's no reason to talk about anything but the reason you don't want to go back to Qaram."

"I told you. My uncle—"

"I heard you the first time. But you're a gold medal winner when it comes to lying, Princess. We both know that. And I'm giving you fair warning that I have no intention of bleeding out in the fucking middle of fucking nowhere just because you're in the mood to spin another fucking fairy tale."

That got her attention. The color swept back into her face; her eyes flashed with topaz fire.

He had never seen her so angry.

So what?

He was the one who was angry.

Hell, he was furious. At her. At himself. At how close he'd come to letting her make a fool of him all over again just a few minutes ago.

"You have no right to speak to me that way!"

"Forgive me, Your Highness, but I don't give a crap about royal protocol."

"You know that's not what I mean! What I'm trying to tell you is that I would never, ever—"

"Never what? Lie to me?" Dec barked out a laugh. Then he turned his back to her and started walking.

6

They reached the edge of the forest.

Tall grass stretched ahead of them, all the way to the rocks and a small pond. The horse tossed its head and snorted. It would have gone forward if Dec hadn't stopped it.

"I agree," he said as he stroked the animal's neck. "The place looks pretty good to me too. Just give me a couple of minutes to check things out." He turned to Annie and his tone of voice went from soft to harsh. "Remember what I said. Stay put until I signal."

Annie clicked her heels together. "Aye aye, Lieutenant."

"Very amusing."

"Yessir."

Dec's eyes narrowed. "In case you haven't figured it out, Princess, this isn't a game."

Her expression darkened. "Do you really think you have to tell me that?"

No. Probably not. On the other hand, until he had

all the pieces of the puzzle, he couldn't be certain about anything.

"If anything goes wrong," he said brusquely, "you get on that horse and ride out of here. Understood?"

"Understood, sir."

Dammit, what was this nonsense? Where was the sweet, soft-spoken Annie he'd known in the past? The last thing he needed was to have to deal with a smartass.

"I hope so, because I sure as shit won't have time to worry about you. Go that?"

"Got it," she said. "Sir."

Part of him wanted to tell her she was making him mad, but what for? She already knew that. It was the reason she was taunting him.

Part of him wanted something entirely different: To haul her into his arms and show her who was in charge here—and what kind of man would that make him? He wasn't into the me Tarzan, you Jane school of thought, and he sure as hell wasn't into showing a woman who was in charge by sexually dominating her.

Although a little domination in bed could be fun, if that was what a man and a woman wanted.

He had no idea what Annie wanted in bed.

How could he when he'd never had her in his bed except to hold her and comfort her with kisses, not with sex.

Not with his hands clasping hers high above her head, his weight bearing down on her, her legs wrapped around his hips as he lost himself inside her...

A shudder ripped through him.

Terrific. All kinds of bad guys were after them and he was standing here with his head up his ass.

"Take the reins," he said sharply. "And remember what I said. Stay right here. Do not move until and unless you see me signal. If things go bad, do not, absolutely do *not* do anything stupid. Just get on the horse and ride for your life. Am I being clear?"

Her eyes glittered with defiance. "Crystal," she said.

He stared at her. Idiot that he was, he wanted to kiss her. But he didn't have to because she stepped up close, rose on her toes, clasped his head with her hands and put her mouth against his.

Even now, sweaty and dirty, she tasted like honey, just as she always had.

Even now, with danger all around them, he wanted to gather her against him and take the kiss deeper.

But she stepped back, and so did he.

Then she snapped off a salute.

He wanted to laugh. Or take her down to the ground and make love to her until until this little bit of the world spun off into space and shot past the sun.

For now, the best he could do was cradle his automatic rifle and start moving stealthily out of the trees.

A SOFT BREEZE ruffled the knee-high grass.

Dec took his time making his way through it, every sense on high alert. As a SEAL and then as a STUD, he'd learned to listen as much as look, to be aware of all the sounds around him.

The sounds here were positive. Bird calls. Insect songs. A good indication that nobody was waiting in ambush. Still, he wasn't about to take anything for granted.

By the time he reached the rocky escarpment, he knew they'd found exactly the right place to spend the night. The rocks formed a natural stone wall, solid and impenetrable, that rose at least twenty feet above the ground.

Quick exploration showed him a bonus. A cave, cut deep into the rock. He checked for signs of life, human or animal. Except for bones that looked as if they'd been there for years, the area was clear.

Outside the cave, there were a couple of stands of young trees with enough downed branches to provide an easy source of kindling and firewood. The pond looked clean, but he had water purification tablets and he intended to use them just to play things safe.

Dec waved Annie in.

He watched her as she made her way across the meadow.

Her gait was steady, but as she drew nearer, he could see that her face was flushed with exertion. Her forehead and chin were streaked with dirt. Her camo pants were torn and there was a rip in the sleeve of her sweater.

She'd been through more bad stuff in a handful of days than most people would face in their lifetimes, and no matter how many questions he had, he'd been a goddamn badass in the way he'd dealt with her.

The least she deserved now was as much of a meal as he could manage and a night's rest. His interrogation could wait until morning.

He walked through the meadow to meet her.

"You okay?" he said.

She nodded. "I'm fine."

Dec took the horse's reins from her and as they headed towards the rocks, he thought about the women he knew, especially the ones who hung out at the Landing Zone in hopes of hooking up with guys from the Units. The blonde, for instance, the one he'd brought home with only—what was it? One day ago? Two days ago?

He'd lost touch with real-world time.

The blonde and the others like her were all the same.

Crop tops and tiny skirts. Nosebleed stilettos Perfect hair. Perfect makeup.

Perfect availability.

A few beers. A little light banter. Some time on the dance floor. Next stop, bed.

He'd never been much on overnights. Bring a woman home, fine. Do your thing, smile, put her into a taxi or drive her home if she hadn't brought her own car. Take her to her place, that was fine too. Simpler, actually. You could always check your watch, say it was getting late, and then you were g one.

The key was not to let things drag on or you could find yourself facing the I'm-gonna-make-you-breakfast routine, that pseudo-domestic intimacy he wanted no part of.

Not that he was a complete boor.

He liked women. He had no wish to hurt their feelings. Sometimes, he sent flowers the next day, but the big thing was getting on with his life.

Still, he'd ended up trapped in morning rituals enough times to know it could take a woman an hour to get herself ready for the world.

The glop they put on their faces. The stuff they used on their eyes. He'd once had the misfortune of seeing a woman contour her face.

Contour her face.

With all those brushes and all those little pans of goop, she could have contoured a map of the world.

And then the what-shall-I-wear bit. Yank a thousand things out of the closet. Toss them on the bed. Hold them up in front of the mirror. Try them on. Discard them.

"It's just the way babes are," Nick Romano had said one night when they were BS-ing, killing time, waiting for darkness to fall before they headed into an Iraqi village to deal with a problem.

"And a good thing, too," Aidan had added. "Because if you ever saw them without all the war paint, you'd just keep walkin'."

Everybody had laughed, Dec included.

Except, it wasn't true.

Annie had spent lots of nights at his place. In the morning, she'd never bothered with any of that stuff and she'd still been the most beautiful woman he'd ever known.

Even now, dirty, exhausted, wearing things that were torn and tattered and mud-stained...even now, she was lovely.

More than lovely.

Everything about her said she was strong and capable, that she could survive whatever life threw at her, and, God, he wanted to take her in his arms, tell her —tell her—

He came to an abrupt stop and thrust the reins at her.

"Water the horse," he said briskly. "You can do that, right?"

She gave him a look that questioned his IQ level.

"Of course. I can also unsaddle him."

"Fine. Do that."

"I can also tether him, assuming you have some sort of line in that pack of yours."

He tried not to show his surprise. "In fact," he said, digging into the pack and coming up with a long length of paracord, "I do. Tether him near the cave."

"Glad you told me that," she said briskly, "or I might have set him up on the far side of the meadow."

Dec's gaze narrowed. "Dammit, woman—"

Shit. He was talking to her back. Okay. Just as well. He had a lot to do before nightfall, which he figured was maybe a couple of hours away.

Like trying to contact Recovery Base.

Like collecting firewood and laying a fire.

Like scouting out the area.

Like figuring out what to do about their sleeping arrangements.

It was going to get cold. And he had one thermal blanket.

Only one.

He could be a gentleman, let her have the blanket while he froze his ass off—except freezing his ass off wasn't the real issue.

The real issue was going to be lying next to her, either on top of that blanket or under it, and not touching her all through the long, dark night.

THE SUN WAS SETTING.

Brushstrokes of color shading from deepest vermillion to the palest pink hung in the sky.

Annie sat within the shelter of the cave, her arms wrapped around her knees, staring into the oncoming night.

Declan had tried to use his satphone, but it hadn't worked. He'd spent a few minutes pressing buttons and muttering under his breath before he'd tossed the thing aside and turned his attention to lighting a fire with some kindling and what he'd told her was a ferro rod.

She'd had to ask twice before he'd told her what the little tool was called.

Obviously, he was not eager to talk to her.

So be it.

The fire felt good even though he'd built it small.

She knew it was to avoid making it visible at a distance. After that, he'd said he was going to scout the area.

"I'll be back," he'd told her.

She'd almost said that Arnold Schwarzenegger had used the same line, but he was gone before she could work up the energy.

Annie sighed.

She was tired, dirty and hungry. But for the first time in months, she felt safe.

Which was, she knew, abjectly ridiculous.

They weren't safe. They were in deep trouble. *Ass-deep in shit*, she'd once heard one of the guys in Declan's unit say about some mission in the past, and right now she couldn't think of a more accurate description of their situation.

Men who wanted to capture her and kill Declan were after them. The outlaws who'd kidnapped her? Her uncle? The horrid king he'd sold her to? The terrorist her kidnappers had sold her to?

Annie shuddered.

No. She wasn't going to think about any of that. Not tonight. She had little doubt that they were all out there somewhere, searching for Declan and her.

Still, she felt...Well, maybe *safe* wasn't quite the right word, but it was close enough. The rocky cliff at their backs offered some sense of security. So did the cave. And the fire. There was something wonderfully atavistic about a fire.

All those things were a comfort.

But nothing was as much a comfort as Declan.

All through the endless climb up the mountain,

riding behind him with her arms around him, her body pressed to his...She'd been frightened, yes. Terrified. But the feel of him in her arms, the heat of him, the strength...

Annie closed her eyes.

How she'd missed him! She'd dreamed of him at night, thought of him during the day, always wondering what he felt about her, believed about her.

She had never dared imagine seeing him again.

And then the shock of finding he was beside her in that awful shed, hearing his voice, feeling his lips on hers and knowing it was not a dream, that he was real, that he had come to save her...

That he despised her.

A soft whisper of despair rose in her throat.

Of course, he despised her. She'd vanished from his life and when she'd reappeared, it was as someone else, a woman he'd never known before...

"Okay."

She looked up. Declan stood in the mouth of the cave, water bottles slung over his shoulders, a batch of reeds and leaves in his arms, a knotted bandana in one hand.

"We'll be okay until morning."

He dumped the reeds and leaves on the cave floor. The floor was relatively smooth, made that way by people and animals over the centuries.

"The reeds and leaves will make a decent bed."

She nodded. "Fine."

"I have a thermal blanket. You'll be warm."

"What about you?"

He shrugged. "I'll be good." He sat down cross-legged opposite her. "Supper time."

"More energy bars?"

"MREs. Meals Ready to Eat. If you thought those energy bars were good, you're gonna love the MREs."

His lips twitched. Was he going to smile? Best not to get her hopes up. Instead, she poked at the knotted bandana.

"What's in there?"

"Open it and take a look."

She unknotted the ends of the cotton square, looked at the contents, then looked at Declan. "Wineberries?" she said with delight.

"Uh huh. They're pretty dried out—they've been around for a while—but they'll still make a good-tasting tea."

"And...Are those cattail corms?"

Dec raised one eyebrow. "Correct on all counts."

Annie smiled. "My mother was into wild plants. Edible wild plants. My father used to tease her about it. 'I'm the barbarian,' he'd say. 'You're the debutante. You're supposed to know all about fine wine and caviar, and I'm supposed to be the expert on foraging for food.'"

Declan looked at her. Then he picked up a long stick and poked at the fire.

"A barbarian who just happened to be the ruler of a wealthy kingdom."

His tone was neutral. The look in his eyes wasn't. Annie met his gaze, flushed and looked away. Why on earth had she mentioned her parents?

"And mom. The girl from—what was it? Smith? Vassar? Barnard?'

"Smith," Annie said in a small voice. "That was where she met my father. He'd come to endow a building You know. He'd provided the backing for..."

Dec laughed.

"No need to explain endowing to me, Princess. My old man endowed a building too. A chicken coop he turned into a studio. Only problem was, we really needed that coop. Without it, the hens laid their eggs every which place and if the foxes didn't find 'em, the snakes did."

Annie raised her head. "Declan. I know you're angry—"

"Angry? Me? Fuck, no. What've I got to be angry about?"

"Hurt, then. And—"

"Is that what you think? That you hurt me?"

Dec set aside the stick, grabbed his pack and began taking things out of it. A small metal pot. A metal cup. Two packages that were the MREs.

A map.

"I know I hurt you," she said. "But you have to understand that I—"

"You didn't. Hurt me, that is. And I don't have to understand a thing, Your Highness."

He spread the map on his crossed legs. Firelight played over his face, making him look tough and mysterious.

Annie swallowed hard.

He didn't look tough and mysterious; he *was* tough

and mysterious. Tough in the best possible way, with that strong, hard body and all those lean muscles; mysterious because she had no idea what he was thinking—except to be pretty sure that if it was about her, it was nothing good.

"Declan?"

"Hmm?"

What are you thinking? Is it about me? Do you hate me? I couldn't stand it if you hated me.

"Do you know where we are?"

He looked at her, then at the map. "Yes. We're on top of a mountain."

"I mean," she said carefully, "do you know *where* we are. In Syria? Tharsalonia? Qaram?"

"No."

"No what? No, we're not in any of those places?"

"No, I don't know where we are. I have an idea, but not enough data to be sure."

She nodded. She remembered how careful he was about data when he'd hacked into a bunch of Top Secret files to help Chay Olivieri find the man who'd been stalking Bianca, who was now Chay's wife.

Precise. Goal-oriented. Committed to facts.

Was that part of the reason she'd never told him the truth about herself? Because the facts that had brought her into his life were too ugly to share?

She cleared her throat. "I—I'm sorry I got you into this mess."

"You didn't get me into anything. My unit was assigned to handle the situation."

The situation. Surely, she was more than that to him.

"Declan?"

He looked up again, a scowl on his face. "What now?"

"I know you must have questions…"

"The only questions I have are the ones that deal with getting us out of here."

"I meant—I meant that you must also have questions about—about me."

"Why would I have questions about you? I know all I need to know. You're some kind of hot prize with a lot of guys competing to get past me so they can win you."

She flinched.

Okay. He'd been a little rough, but he was in no mood to be kind. Yes, he'd wanted to hear her story, but making the fire, then foraging for whatever food he could find had given him time to think.

He didn't need to hear her story. All he needed was to contact Recovery Base, arrange for a pickup and make it clear that for whatever reason, the princess didn't want to be returned to Qaram or sent to Tharsalonia.

He didn't have to know the reason.

What would be the point?

She was a twenty-first century Scheherazade, and he was living proof that a man could fall for the tales she told and, in the process, lose his grasp of reality.

He'd never thought about being with one woman to the exclusion of all others until she'd come into his life, and look what that ridiculous idea had done for him. Weeks of missing her, then trying to get over her, all of it leading to that disaster with the blonde a couple of night ago, hell, the disasters before that...

He was in the prime of life, and he couldn't get fucking laid because Her Highness the Princess Anoushka had taken up residence in his head?

It was like the punchline to a bad joke.

And what if the story she told him this time was true? Forget that. What if it sounded true? What if he believed that her uncle had sold her as if she were a piece of property?

Dec felt a stab of rage in his gut, followed by an immediate sense of calm.

Simple.

He'd have to kill her uncle. Her uncle, and the would-be bridegroom who she said had bought her. Eliminating them would move to the top of his To Do list and he'd need to deal with the planning and the doing, and what that would mean was that he'd lose focus.

He could not permit himself to lose focus.

Getting her to safety was the priority. He needed to be able to think clearly, without emotion, for that to happen. She didn't want to go back to Qaram? Her business, not his.

His business was contacting Recovery Base, setting up a new extraction location and getting to it. As for her tale of woe about Qaram—no problem. He'd tell his communications liaison that the lady wanted to be taken, well, wherever she wanted to be taken. Paris. London. New York. Hell, Disneyland.

So, no. He didn't need to hear her story. He didn't want to hear her story. He wanted to figure out where the fuck they were and then get through to base...

He wanted this to be over.

Annie—the princess—got to her feet.

"If you need to pee," Dec said, without lifting his gaze from the map, "don't go very far. Right outside the cave is best."

"Thank you for that heartwarming advice."

Okay. That made him look up. What he saw wasn't good. Her eyes were hot, her mouth was a tight line. He wasn't particularly good at reading women, this one especially, but even he could tell that the lady wasn't happy.

"Just trying to be helpful, Your Majesty. You want to risk walking into a wolf or a badger, be my guest."

"Do not call me that!"

"Sorry. I guess I'm not up on court protocol. Your Highness. How's that?"

"Stop it!"

"Stop what?"

"Stop acting as if we're strangers."

A muscle knotted in his jaw. "But that's what we are. Strangers."

"We aren't! You can't pretend we were never—we were never—"

"We were never what? I mean, how would you define our relationship? I thought we were Dec and Annie. Wrong. Turns out we were the fall guy and the princess."

"You were never that. And I wasn't a princess. I hate

those titles. I always did. I never liked hearing people use them. And with you, especially—"

"With me, especially, you didn't use a title. I get that. It was part of the act. No title. No demand that I bow in your presence or walk a couple of steps behind you. It was too much fun playing at being a sweet little innocent, all alone in the world."

"I wasn't playing," Annie said fiercely. "How can you even think such a thing? You know me."

"I sure as hell know you now. So do us both a favor and keep quiet. I have to do some thinking. You have to keep your strength up." He jerked his chin at the bandana and the MREs. "No filet mignon or lobster on the menu .Not up to your regal standards, but it's the best I can do."

Annie felt the sting of angry tears in the backs of her eyes. "Do you hate me so much?"

"I'm sorry to disappoint you, but the simple truth is that I don't feel anything for you one way or the—"

A cattail corm whizzed by his head. Dec looked up. Annie glared at him, breathing rapid, eyes flashing.

His vision blurred.

He wanted to grab her and shake her.

Or grab her and haul her down on top of him, kiss her until she sobbed with wanting him, until her hands were all over him...

Shit.

He dragged his gaze back to the map.

A couple of minutes went by. Then she spoke in a shaky voice. "The sooner this is over, the better."

Apparently, it was her exit line because she spun on her heel and marched deeper into the cave.

Dec folded the map and stared at the fire until all he could see were flaming points of light.

She wanted to sulk? Let her. Why would he give a damn?

She'd gotten one thing right. The sooner this was over, the better. In the meantime, he had to keep up his strength.

Not just his.

Hers too.

He put the map away, filled the small pot with water and set it over the fire. Then he peeled and sliced up some of the cattail corms. Those, wineberry tea and the MREs would do for dinner. Not a gourmet mea, but it would be filling and, according to Uncle Sam, it would also be nutritious.

One small problem.

He had no appetite

And Annie was still back there in the darkness of the cave. So what? She could do what she wanted.

The water was boiling. Dec took it off the fire and dumped a handful of wineberries into it. The smell that rose from the pot was pleasant and the tea might have some minor medicinal benefit. Annie had probably known that. She said she'd learned about wild edibles from her mother.

She'd smiled when she talked about her parents, but she never smiled when she mentioned her uncle Cyrus. If anything, her expression always turned wary.

More than wary.

Frightened.

Okay. Maybe the uncle was a shit. Yeah, but if he was, it had nothing to do with him.

The berries had been steeping for a couple of minutes. Long enough.

Dec peered some of the tea into the cup—he only had the one and they'd have to share it. He blew on the steaming liquid and took a careful sip. Man, it was hot. Yeah, well, that was good. He wanted something warm in his belly. It was black as ink outside and the temperature was taking a nosedive. The fire helped, but he'd kept it small rather than run the risk of it being visible.

And just how long was the princess going to do the sulking routine?

She had to be getting cold without the heat from the fire to chase the chill of the mountain night. She had to know that she needed food. Whatever else she was, she wasn't stupid. She surely realized that their survival depended as much on their physical well-being as on his ability to protect her.

And, dammit, letting her go hungry and thirsty, letting her core body temp drop as it well might, was not any kind of protection. He needed to be in shape to get her out of here. She needed to be in shape to follow his orders. No way could he let her delay this mission.

Same as she, he wanted it to be finished with it, fast.

Dec got to his feet. "Princess?" No answer. He rolled his eyes, got his flashlight and started walking back into the cave. "Pity party's over."

Still nothing.

Hell.

He'd checked for animal life, but maybe he'd missed something. A snake. Even some kind of big venomous bug. He'd been on missions in this part of the world before. There were spiders here that were the size of a man's hand. Or maybe there was another passageway that he hadn't noticed. He'd been in caves that ran for miles and miles.

"Anoushka," he said, raising his voice, "where are you?"

Silence.

"Goddammit, Your Highness, what the fuck do you think you're doing? I told you, the party's over." Dec turned in a tight circle, casting the light over the cave walls. His heart began racing. Jesus. If something had happened to her, if she was hurt, if he never held her in his arms again...

She stepped out of the shadows.

He caught her in the full beam of the flashlight. Tears had left tracks on her dirt-smudged face.

"Annie," he growled. "Goddammit, Annie..."

"I hate you, Declan," she said. "I really, really hate—"

And then, at long last, she was in his arms.

7

Dec groaned, gathered her hard against him and captured her mouth with his. The taste of her was all he could ever want.

She was all he could ever want.

She rose to him. Wound her arms around his neck. He swept his hands up her back, buried them in her hair.

"Kiss me," she whispered, "kiss me, never stop kissing—"

Never. He would never stop kissing her.

But it wasn't enough.

It had never been enough, but he'd been strong in the past; he'd lived on her kisses, on the feel of her in his arms.

Not tonight.

He needed more.

He needed her.

And he couldn't have her, couldn't take her, she would draw back, he knew she would, she'd do what she'd always done, take her lips from his, dig her face into his throat or his shoulder, make it apparent that she didn't want to go further and he would honor that, Jesus, he had to honor it...

He lifted her off her feet.

She wrapped her legs around his hips.

He could feel the heat of her against his dick. His stone-hard dick.

"Annie," he said, the single word a whispered warning, "Annie..."

She ground her pelvis against his.

There was no other way to describe it.

She was grinding against him. Moving against him. Moaning and moving and, God, he couldn't do this, he was only human, they had to stop, *she* had to stop or he was going to strip her pants off, yank down his zipper, bury himself inside her...

Ah, Christ!

She was tugging at his sweater. Trying to drag it up his body, then shoving her hands under it and putting them on his chest, her palms hot against his skin.

Declan shuddered under that soft, exciting touch. He clasped her wrists. Stilled her hands. Bent his head and lay his forehead against hers.

"Annie." His voice was low. Raw. "Annie, if you keep touching me...I won't be able to stop.'"

"Please," she said, "Declan, please please please please..."

A growl rose in his throat.

He carried her through the cave, to the fire.

Went down with her on the leafy bed.

She rolled into his arms, her mouth still fused to his, one of her legs thrown over his, her hands pulling at his sweater again until he tore it off and tossed it aside.

"You're beautiful," she whispered.

He gave a broken laugh. "You're the one who's beautiful, sweetheart. You're the most beautiful woman in the world."

"I want to be beautiful for you. I want to be everything for you."

"You are," he said, framing her face with his hands. "You always were. You always will be."

He kissed her. She moaned and pulled back and for a heartbeat, he thought he was going to die, that she was going to stop him from loving her.

"Declan," she whispered "Undress me."

He could hear the thunder of his blood.

"Are you sure, sweetheart?"

She clasped his hands. Brought them to her. "Undress me," she said, and whatever faint hope of restraint he might have had left was gone.

He undressed her slowly.

His hands trembled.

Her sweater first. It was the one he'd given her, military issue, voluminous and rough.

What was beneath it almost stopped his heart.

Annie was beneath it. Pure Annie. No bra. No T-shirt. Just Annie, her skin the color of pale gold, her breasts high and small and perfect, God, perfect, the nipples a sweet, delicate pink.

He bent to her. Kissed the slope of her breasts.

Trailed the tip of his tongue over that warm, tender flesh.

She moaned. Trembled. Whispered his name. And when he cupped her breasts, gently kissed the tightly furled buds, she cried out and writhed beneath him.

Gently, he rolled one nipple between his fingers.

She arched towards him, sobbing.

He closed his lips around her other nipple. Sucked on it.

Her hands fisted in his hair as her cry rose into the night. "Declan," she sobbed, "Declan, Declan, Declan..."

He kissed her mouth, her throat, felt the race of her pulse beneath his kisses and then his lips closed around the tip of one breast again and her sobs, her breathless little cries, her body moving against his...

He could feel what was happening to him.

The tightening of his balls. The sense that he was going to explode.

No. Not yet. Not yet...

"Please," she whispered, "please."

His hands shook as he unzipped her pants. "Lift up," he said hoarsely, and when she did, he pulled the pants down to her ankles, stopped to yank off her boots, then dragged the pants off and threw them aside.

Her panties were lace. White lace, but they were demure, almost modest. Carefully, he drew them down her thighs, her calves, her ankles, groaning as he exposed her to his eyes. The gentle curve of her hips, the delicacy of her belly button, the soft dark curls between her thighs.

He bent to her, kissed her belly button, kissed his way lower, lower, put his mouth against those curls. Her hands flew up to stop him.

"No," she whispered, "you can't, you can't..."

He caught her wrists, nuzzled against her. Her thighs parted and he inhaled her scent, put his mouth to her and kissed her.

"God," she sobbed, "oh God..."

He found her with his tongue, tasted the sweet essence of her. Woman. Passion. Everything he had ever dreamed or wanted.

She moaned. And then she cried out and bucked against his mouth, and he knew he couldn't wait any longer, couldn't wait, couldn't wait...

He got to his feet. Somehow managed to kick off his boots. Unzipped his fly, shoved down his pants and his shorts, and came down to her again.

"Annie," he said hoarsely.

She raised her eyes to his.

"Declan," she answered, and he knew that no matter what lay ahead of them, he would never forget the way she said his name, the way she opened her arms to him.

He said her name again.

Then, slowly, slowly, his eyes never leaving hers, he eased inside her.

She was hot. Wet. Tight. She was silk and he was steel.

She was the only thing in life that mattered.

His vision blurred. His heartbeat accelerated. She was lifting herself to him, her breath coming in tight little puffs. Her hands clutched his biceps...

Suddenly, she went rigid. "Wait," she gasped.

And then he felt it.

The barrier.

His Annie was a virgin. Sweet Jesus. A virgin.

How could he have forgotten that she would, damn right, be a virgin?

At first, the thought of what she was giving him— her innocence, the very symbol of her womanhood— made him the most special man in the world.

It took barely a second for that idea to crash and burn.

She was a virgin, and that explained everything,

Why she'd always pulled back in the past.

Why she'd seemed so innocent.

Hell, it was because she *was* innocent, and in this part of the world a woman was expected to save herself for the man she married.

The woman he'd thought of as his had been doing exactly that, saving herself, just waiting for the day she would take a husband—and she'd been on her way to do that when she was kidnapped.

Reality came hard and fast.

This wasn't a bed, it was a pile of leaves. This wasn't an idyll on a mountaintop, it was a moment torn out of time.

And the woman lying beneath him wasn't his. She never had been; she never would be.

Amazing, how quickly desire could die.

Dec rolled away, got to his feet, grabbed for his pants and yanked them on.

"Declan?"

He didn't look at her. Instead, he scooped up her clothes and tossed them to her.

"Get dressed."

"Are you upset because I've never—because I've never been with a man? I know I should have told you—"

"It's late. I need to check on the horse."

"Declan. Wait..."

Dec strode into the night, but he didn't go very far. He sank back against the face of the cliff and rubbed his hands over his face.

Jesus, he had to be crazy. He needed to get her out of his head and instead, he'd almost planted her there permanently. He'd never taken a woman's virginity, but he knew damn well it was the kind of thing that a man would not forget. It would have stayed with him, probably forever.

That was the last thing he needed.

The Princess of Qaram, inside his skull for the rest of his life.

Women were for fun. For sex, for laughter, for good times. And if some guys found more than that, well, good for them, but he'd never figured on being one of them.

Forever wasn't on his agenda.

And then Annie had come into his life and everything had changed.

She'd filled empty spaces in his head, his heart,

fuck, in his soul, empty spaces that he'd never even known existed. Then she'd left, and all his empty places had been empty again.

He'd told her she hadn't hurt him.

What a lie.

She'd hurt him beyond anything he could have imagined, but he'd been getting over it. Of course he'd been getting over it.

Which was why he didn't want her in his life again.

What he wanted was her out and gone. Then maybe he could get back to being himself, Declan Sanchez, a guy who lived for risk and excitement and—

And what?

Hell.

And for getting this mission accomplished.

He'd lost sight of that. The questions he hadn't asked had to be asked. Why didn't she want to go back to Qaram? Whose prize was the Princess Anoushka supposed to be?

He took a long, deep breath. Then he turned and went back inside the cave.

Annie had put on her clothes. She was sitting as she had been earlier, with her arms wrapped around her knees.

Dec cleared his throat. "Annie."

"Go away."

"Listen. About what happened—"

"Nothing happened," she said in a tone cold enough to freeze water.

"Yeah. Right. I mean...Let's put that aside."

She looked up at him. "Trust me," she said in that same icy voice. "I already have."

Man, she was furious. Okay. Maybe she had the right to be angry, but that didn't mean he didn't still need information.

"You have to tell me what's going on."

"I don't *have* to tell you a damned thing."

Okay. Enough. Dec reached down, grasped her shoulders and hauled her to her feet.

"You want to get out of this alive? Then you need to tell me what I'm into here."

"What *you're* into?" Her chin lifted. "Why am I not surprised that you think this is all about you?"

"Look, I know you tried to explain the situation to me and I cut you off. I was stupid."

Her smile was all teeth. "At least we agree on something."

"I have to see all the puzzle pieces if I'm going to get us out of this situation."

"My uncle stole my father's throne. He wants to invade Suwaith. He needs Tharsalonia's cooperation. To get it, he sold me to the Tharsalonian king, but somehow Altair Amjad, the Great Deliverer of his band of cutthroats, decided he wanted me to legitimatize his not-so-sterling reputation. Those are the puzzle pieces." Annie shoved against Declan's chest. "Now get the hell away from me, Lieutenant Sanchez. And stay away."

"It's too late for that. I'm here. You're here. Goddammit, you've been here, inside me, since we met on that beach." Dec's hands slid to her elbows. "I want the truth, Annie. All of it, from that first day to the day you vanished and straight through to now. Tell me why you lied to me, why you figured it was okay to string me along and then walk out of my life without so much as a *Goodbye, good luck, it was fun.* You hear me? I want the story from A to Z, with not a goddamn word left out."

He was shaking her. He hadn't meant to shake her, but he was hot with rage, with anger...

With pain.

And Annie... Ah, dear God, Annie was sobbing.

He'd hurt her and God, he'd never wanted to hurt her, to disappoint her, to do anything but make her happy.

What he'd just done—starting to make love to her, then walking away... Jesus. He couldn't believe he'd done such a despicable thing.

And why? Because he was jealous of a man she'd already told him she didn't want to marry?

His head kept telling him she was lying, but his heart knew the truth. She wasn't capable of lying. If she had lied to him, it had been because she'd truly believed she had no other choice.

How terrible her life must have been for her to have been afraid of letting him in.

Dec groaned and gathered her into his arms. She fought him, but not for long. A heartbeat later she had her arms around him and her face buried in his throat.

"Baby," he said brokenly, "Annie. Forgive me." He held her against him, stroking his hand down her back, cradling her against his body, rocking her gently in his arms. "I think I went crazy when you left me."

Annie lifted her tear-stained face and kissed him.

"I never wanted to leave you, " she whispered. "Why would I have left the man I love?"

Could you actually feel your heart fill with joy? Declan bent his head and kissed her.

"I'm in love with you," he said. "I can't remember a time I wasn't in love with you."

Tears filled her eyes. "I never thought I'd hear you say those words."

He kissed her again. Gently at first, and then she made a soft little sigh of surrender, of desire, and he changed the angle of the kiss. Deepened it, and she moaned and stroked her hand down his spine.

He undressed her again, even as she undressed him. Slowly, this time, with soft caresses and kisses as each bit of skin was bared.

When she was naked, the sight of her took his breath away.

She was everything he had dreamed, everything he'd wanted. Her delicate breasts. Her narrow waist. Her gently rounded hips and long legs.

He would never get enough of having her in his arms.

He drew her down to their bed of leaves and she opened her arms to him.

"Come into me," she said, and as he captured her mouth with his, he sank into her, gritting his teeth with the effort of taking her slowly, of not hurting her, of giving her time to adjust to him.

He was big. He knew that. The size of his dick had always been a source of what he realized was foolish male pride, but the women he'd been with were always experienced.

Annie wasn't, and he was afraid he might cause her pain.

And, dammit, he was. He had to be, judging by the breathless little whisper that went from her mouth to his.

Dec went still.

"I'm hurting you," he said hoarsely.

She shook her head. "No. Yes. Declan. Don't stop. Don't—"

He groaned and slid deeper.

She said his name. Wound her arms around his neck as he slipped his hands under her ass and lifted her to him.

"Oh," she whispered, "oh oh oh..."

He was inside her now, not all the way, not far enough, but despite what she'd said, he knew he had to be hurting her, she was so tight and he was so big. He was shaking; it was hard, so hard not to take her completely, not to make her his after all the days and weeks of waiting...

"Declan," she said, and before he realized what she was going to do, she raised her hips and impaled herself on his erection.

The world tilted.

She gave a sweet, soft moan and rocked against him, and whatever control remained to him was gone.

He drove into her.

She sobbed his name. Bit his lip. Fisted her hands in his hair as he claimed her. Wrapped her legs tightly around his hips so she could meet each thrust of his body.

He was going to come.

No. Not yet. Not yet...

But she was with him.

He could feel it happening.

The tensing of her muscles. The contraction of her silken walls. She was coming for him, coming with him, and somehow he managed to hang on until she threw back her head and screamed—and then he let go of everything: the loneliness, the despair, the endless weeks without her, and fell over the edge of the universe with his Annie in his arms.

8

_____

At first, the world was a blur. Then, gradually, he became aware of things. The slowing beat of his heart. The dampness of sweat on his skin.

Annie, lying beneath him.

He stirred. She sighed. He started to ease himself off her—he had to outweigh her by seventy, eighty pounds—but she made a whisper of protest and held him closer.

He smiled and buried his face in her hair...

And realized he hadn't worn a condom.

What the hell...?

It was the first time in his entire life that he hadn't. At age sixteen, in the hayloft of Sally Webster's barn, he'd had his first sexual experience that didn't involve his own right hand and, yes, he'd worn a condom.

He'd never not used one, and there'd been no reason not to use one tonight. He had condoms in his gear. STUDs especially got ranked on about it, but Special Ops forces had long ago figured out that condoms weren't only for sex—they could also hold life-giving liquids like water in an emergency.

He knew he should be upset about the condom thing...but how he could he be upset over anything when what he'd just experienced had been so fantastic? There had to be a better word, but right now, *fantastic* would have to do.

Carefully, he rolled onto his side with Annie in his arms. "Honey?"

She sighed, her breath warm against his throat. "Mmm?"

Such a lovely sound, that whispered "Mmm."

"Sweetheart. Are you okay?"

"I'm fine," she said, laying her hand over his heart.

"That's it?" he said teasingly. "You're fine?"

She drew back a little, titled her head so she could see his face, and smiled. "Are you looking for compliments, Lieutenant?"

He grinned. "Well, if you want to toss one my way..."

She laughed and snuggled closer. He closed his eyes and drank in the hot, silky feel of her body.

Dammit.

She didn't know that all this skin- to-skin contact, the delicate pressure of her hips against his, the sweet rub of her nipples against his chest, was starting to drive him crazy. He was getting hard. And this was too fast, too soon.

Not for him.

For her.

She was new to this. She needed a chance to rest.

She sighed and put her leg over his thigh. He could feel her heat. And, man, he was going from hard to harder.

"I'm more than fine," she said. "I'm wonderful."

"Yes," he said solemnly, "you are."

She blushed. He loved that blush, especially while her hand was moving over his chest. Down over his abs....

"I never imagined it would be like this," she whispered. "Being with you...I never thought..."

"No. Neither did I." Gently, he brushed his lips over hers. " I always knew it would be incredible, but this— this was..." He cleared his throat. "Honey. I didn't use a condom. I just—I should have, but I didn't think."

Just for a second, her eyes seemed to darken. Then she smiled and traced the outline of his mouth with the tip of her finger.

"It's alright."

"Yeah. But..." He cleared his throat again. "I'm clean. You need to know that. And just in case... I'm here for you, princess. I'll always be here."

There it was again. That swift darkening of her eyes. He knew what she was thinking, because he had the same thought.

They had created their own world, but it wouldn't last. Reality was out there, searching for them. And it would find them; they both understood that.

But not yet.

Not just yet.

And he wanted her again.

There was only one solution. He had to get up, move away from her. There were things he could do to keep busy. Get the thermal blanket from his pack. Check the horse again even though it didn't need checking. Make some more tea. Say the alphabet twenty times, count backwards from one hundred...

"Declan?" Annie rose up on her elbow. She leaned over him and her long, dark hair made a silken curtain around his face and hers. "Please. Stop thinking."

He reached up, took a strand of her hair and let it drift through his fingers.

"Am I that easy to read?"

"What we have now...It's more than I'd dare hope for. And I know—I know we're in danger, that what lies ahead is—is unpredictable." She smiled, and he saw the glitter of unshed tears in her eyes. "But for now, we're together. We have each other. I don't want to think about anything else even if it's just for a little while."

He cupped the back of her head and brought her mouth to his for a long, deep kiss.

"We're going to get through this, sweetheart. I swear it to you."

She nodded. "I know you'll do everything you can," she said softly. "For now, though...For now, I just want you to make love to me."

His body's response was swift and unmistakable.

Annie laughed. Her laugh was sexy, husky, purely female, and he loved the sound of it.

He caressed her breasts, licked and sucked her nipples, kissed his way down the length of her body.

She sighed. Moaned. Experimented with touching him, with trailing light kisses down his belly until she reached his engorged dick and he was crazy with the need for release.

Take her, everything in him said, *take her now, hard and fast...*

But he held back.

It was worth it just so he could whisper, "My turn," and roll her on her back.

So he could watch her eyes blur when he tongued her nipples, when he slid his hand between her thighs and stroked her clit, when he moved over her and entered her inch by slow inch, filling her, stretching her until she sobbed his name and he knew he was making her world come apart.

She arched towards him, her cries soft and sweet on the night air as her orgasm begin to claim her.

She was coming because of him.

Because she loved him.

She loved him.

His own vision blurred. He took one last, deep thrust, and when he called out her name, it was with the fierce determination of a warrior.

She was his, and he would kill any man who tried to take her from him.

～

HE LEFT her only to dispose of the condom, get the thermal blanket from his gear and spread it over her, then stoke the fire. A pair of owls hooted to each other; somewhere in the distance, an animal howled. There'd once been wolves in this wilderness. Maybe there still were.

By the time he lay down again and gathered her into his arms, she was asleep.

He drew her closer.

He loved holding her. He loved being with her. He loved everything about her and though it came close to scaring the crap out of him, what he truly loved was her.

What kind of fate or destiny, karma or whatever you chose to call it had brought her to him under such seemingly impossible circumstances?

Yeah, but nothing was truly impossible.

He was living proof, otherwise he'd still in New Mexico, maybe working with horses or, more probably, holding down a job at a mine.

Annie burrowed closer. He stroked his hand up and down her back. Despite the blanket, her skin was cool. He dropped a light kiss on her hair and gathered her closer.

She made another of those little *mmm* sounds.

He'd told her he didn't want to hear her story. Not true. He not only wanted to hear it, he needed to hear it. Why had she pretended to be somebody she wasn't? Why had she left him? And what was this stuff about her uncle? The guy sounded like a stand-in for a wicked stepmother. It was a lousy metaphor, but so what?

She needed help and he'd come close to letting his ego keep him from helping her.

Dec yawned.

He was bone-weary. And hungry. She had to be hungry too.

Okay.

Twenty minutes of shut-eye and he'd get up, get dressed, go and check on the horse—one of the best early-warning systems on the planet, as far as he was concerned. Then he'd wake Annie, open the MREs, and then—and then—

And then, he was asleep.

SOMETHING WOKE HIM.

A snort. A low whinny from the horse.

Dec sat up.

It was still dark; the fire had burned down to coals. He could barely see a foot ahead of him.

He waited, listening, every sense on alert. The world had gone silent. No insect sounds. No distant howls or hoots.

The hair on the back of his neck rose.

Somebody was out there. And, yes, now he could hear something moving through the high grass.

He put his lips to Annie's ear and whispered her name. Her eyes flew open and met his.

"Honey. We may have visitors."

She opened her mouth to speak. He shook his head and put his finger against her lips.

"No talking. Just get your clothes on, fast. You got that?"

Her nod was frantic.

"That's my girl," he whispered.

He gave her a quick kiss. Her lips clung to his and it took everything in him to push her gently away.

She dressed quickly. So did he. He opened the snap on the sheath that held his knife, took the safety off his HK MP7.

The horse snorted.

Dec moved quietly forward.

His pulse quickened. Was that the wind? Or was it…

Voices.

Voices. Not the wind. Two men exchanging guttural whispers in a local dialect. He could smell them—the stink of rancid grease and cheap booze drifted to him on the wind. They were still maybe twenty-five, thirty feet away. Scouts, he figured, working miles ahead of the rest of their party.

He and Annie had been found and it was his fault. He had forgotten to be cautious and now her life was at risk.

Annie was crowded against him.

"Two men," she whispered. "One says he'll kill you while the other—"

Dec held up his hand to silence her. Then he clasped her wrist and drew her back from the entrance.

"Just two," he said. "Nothing I can't handle."

"Tell me what to do."

"Move as far back into the cave as possible."

"I don't want to leave you to face them alone. Tell me how I can help."

"You can help by doing what I told you to do."

"Give me a weapon. A knife. A gun. I know how to shoot, Declan. My father taught me."

"Annie, goddammit, we're wasting time."

"I told you, I know how to shoot!"

What had he told himself just a little while ago? She wasn't a liar. Dec nodded, unholstered his Glock and gave it to her. "Just point and pull the trigger. You got that?"

"I've got it."

"We're going to be fine, honey." Nothing like sounding convinced even if you weren't. "Just stay put until I tell you it's safe. Okay?"

"Declan." She took a breath. "Listen to me. If everything goes bad, I'd rather die than go back."

His jaw tightened. What had they done to her? Something awful enough so that she'd sooner lose her life than be captured? And he, fucking asshole that he was, had doubted her story.

"Didn't you hear me? We're going to be fine."

"I know. But—but just in case...You can't let them take me. Do you understand?"

He reached for her, kissed her, looked into her eyes.

"I won't let them take you," he said. "I swear it."

She gave a quick nod.

What he'd told her was the truth. Of course, he

would give his life for hers—and if it came to more than that...If there was no other choice, he'd take her with him into death.

But he had no intention of dying on this day. He'd only just found the woman he loved. He was not going to lose her now.

"Go," he whispered.

She vanished into the darkness of the cave.

Time to move, and move fast.

Dec jammed his gear bag and a couple of lengths of wood under the thermal blanket. It didn't look much like two sleeping people if you got up close, but all he needed was a couple of seconds' diversion.

As quietly as a big cat, he slipped close to the cave entrance, then flattened himself against the rocky wall to one side. He knew they'd come in one at a time, exactly as he would in the same circumstances.

A minute passed. Then two...

The first man came in low. Light from the dying fire glinted on the knife in his hand.

Dec let him get just inside the cave.

Then he stepped forward, wrapped his arm around the guy's neck, drew him up and back, and slit his throat.

The man went down noiselessly. Dec kicked him aside.

One down. One to go.

And there he was. The second guy. Crouched down, moving more cautiously, knife in his outstretched hand.

"Sahir?" he whispered. He stepped inside the cave. Slowly. Very slowly. "Sahir?" he said again.

He grunted when Dec grabbed him, but that was all he managed before Dec's blade slid into the nape of his neck and severed his spinal cord.

He went down like a stone.

Dec waited. Counted off the seconds just to be sure these two were on their own. After a little while, he heard the hooting of the owls and he relaxed.

Nobody else was out there.

He and Annie were alone.

Well, alone except for two corpses.

He squatted down. Checked each for a pulse and found none. One guy had a long scarf wrapped around his head and the lower part of his face; Dec used it to wipe clean the blade of his knife before returning it to its sheath.

"Declan?"

"Annie," he said sharply. "Stay back,"

Too late. She had already seen the bodies. Dec got to his feet, ready to go to her—this was not a pretty sight and he didn't know what to expect. But when he looked at her, what he saw a woman holding his Glock by her side, cool acceptance in her eyes.

He reached for the gun and took it from her.

"The man with the scarf was one of my guards at the kidnapper's camp," she said. "The other was one of my uncle's thugs."

Dec nodded. The flatness of her speech, the expression on her face told him enough to make him regret he'd killed these two bastards as quickly as he had. He wanted to say something clever, something that would help her, but years of training had taken over.

This was not a time to show emotion.

It was time to get the fuck out of Dodge.

"Okay," he said briskly. "We have to get moving."

"What can I do to help?"

He looked over at her. She was standing straight and tall. His throat constricted. How had he gotten so lucky? She was a beautiful woman with the heart of a tigress.

To hell with training. He went to her, pulled her into his arms and kissed her.

"I love you," he said. "I've always loved you and I always will."

She wound her arms around his neck. "It's the same for me," she whispered. "I love you with all my heart."

He held her for a moment. It was hard to let go of her, but he had no way of knowing how close on their heels the men who'd sent the scouts might be. One last quick kiss. Then he told her to fold the blanket and stuff it into his pack along with the uneaten MREs, the pot, the cup and anything else they'd left lying around while he stamped out the remnants of the fire and saddled the horse.

"That's it," he said. moments later. "Let's go."

"What about the bodies?"

"No point in moving them." A muscle knotted in Dec's jaw. "I want whoever sent these clowns to know that this isn't gonna be a walk in the park."

She nodded, but what he saw in her face made him curse, go to her and take her in his arms again.

"Honey, I promise., I'm going to get you out of this."

She buried her face against his chest. "I know you will," she whispered.

Dec kissed her. Held her. Then he led her into the night

9

Dec knew they were deep in the Copper Mountains.

The mountain range was enormous. He'd traveled through it before. From the air, the Coppers looked like a series of dark brown and green folds, one mountain following after the other, interspersed with plateaus and meadows and narrow valleys.

His GPS was gone, probably lost in their wild gallop away from the rescue helicopter. The best he could figure, they were twenty, twenty-five klicks west of the Syrian border, but he wasn't comfortable taking Annie there. North would get them to Turkey. He knew a little about the area and felt better about it, but to go north they'd have to do another two, three days of riding, walking and climbing.

When they'd first set up camp, he'd walked along the base of the cliff, looking for a way to the top. After about half an hour he'd found something that only an optimist could call a path, but it would do.

He just hadn't expected to make the climb in the dark, but he didn't want to use his LED flashlight—why run the risk of putting an illuminated *Here We Are* sign over their heads?

Luckily, the sky was bright with stars and the way up looked to be no more than twenty, thirty feet.

He led the horse up the rocky slope on foot, with Annie scrambling up beside him. The horse was nervous, snorting and tossing its head at the steep angle and uneven footing.

It was a relief to reach the top.

DAWN WAS STILL a few hours away. Dec wanted to put some distance between them and whoever was on their heels before the sun came up.

Decision time. Which way to go?

West towards Syria was the logical choice—but maybe logic wasn't their best bet right now.

"Okay," he said. "Let's take a five minute break."

Annie was breathing hard. She flopped down in the grass beside the horse. Dec got out the water. The MREs would take too much long to heat and eat, but he had a few energy bars left. They had the cattail corms as well. It wasn't much of a meal, but it would do.

When they'd finished eating and drinking, he put everything away and sat down beside Annie.

"There's a town west of us," he said. "It's fair-sized

and the last anybody heard, it's not been the scene of any fighting."

"And that's where we're going?"

He shook his head. "I figure it's where they'll expect us to go." He pointed straight ahead. "The map shows nothing due north between here and Turkey, but I know the area. It's mostly empty country, small farms, lots of sheep and goats. There's a road, a dirt road, just a few klicks ahead. Only the locals use it. It'll take us to the Turkish border and a small market town. I think that's our best bet."

Annie sighed. "All this trouble because of me."

Dec took her hand, brought it to his mouth and kissed it.

"Hey," he said lightly, "the last time I was in this part of the world I spent three days in a ditch with two other guys. We got rained on each night, got baked to a crisp each day, and one of the guys had this, ah, this bowel problem..."

Annie laughed, exactly as he'd hoped she would. He leaned forward and brushed his lips gently over hers.

"Another two, three days at the most, we'll be out of here."

"I just wish, you know, I wish I could turn back the clock, that we were on the beach at your place in Santa Barbara,."

Dec put his arm around her and she rested her head on his shoulder.

"Maybe we can't turn back time, but we can write

the future. We're going to be on that beach again. Together."

"I hope."

"We will be. And you'll give me a hard time about me not using sun screen, the way you always did, and I'll insist I never burn, the way I always did, and when my nose turns bright red you'll stick out your tongue and say *See? I told you so!*"

She drew back a little and smiled. "I never said 'I told you so!'"

"No? Well, you should have." He smiled back at her. Then he drew her close. "We'll be together. We'll be happy. And this time, it will last."

They sat that way for another couple of minutes. Then Annie stirred, raised her head and looked at him.

"Declan. We have to talk."

"I agree. Tonight, after we find a safe place. We'll talk them. I promise."

THEY FOUND THE ROAD—ACTUALLY, it was a ribbon of packed-down dirt—and, as Dec had said it would, it took them north through an area that seemed almost unpopulated.

They saw an occasional farmhouse, always in the distance, and small, wandering herds of sheep and goats.

The only person they saw was an old man with a horse and wagon, and the old guy was actually asleep, his chin on his chest, as the horse clopped slowly past.

Whenever they paused for a break, Dec scanned the vast area all around them with his binoculars. So far, nobody was following them. He saw only more sheep, more goats, and, a couple of times, small herds of horses.

"Kurdish," Annie said.

Dec shook his head. "We're nowhere near Kurdistan."

"It's the name of the breed. There are two kinds of horses in this part of the world. Arabians. And Kurdish. This guy we're riding is probably Kurdish." She patted the animal's flank. "He's big and strong. And handsome."

"Like me," Dec said.

Annie laughed. "Exactly like you."

The satphone still wasn't working. Dec had no idea why. The phone itself seemed okay and it had never failed him before. He'd just have to work around it. Anyway, they'd eventually reach the border and the little market town where he'd find a phone and arrange for extraction the old fashioned way.

The day began to wind down.

Annie was worn out. Everything she'd experienced in the last several days had to be catching up. She hadn't complained , but Dec recognized the signs. The last time they'd taken a break, he'd been startled at how pale she was, and how her hands s trembled when she raised the water bag to her lips.

She needed rest. Real rest. In a bed, with a roof over her head. And real food, or at least a hot MRE.

The bottom line was that he had to find a place to

spend the night and as dangerous as it might be to ride up to a farmhouse and ask for shelter, it would be even more dangerous to wait to do it until it was dark.

Then, unexpectedly, their fortunes changed.

Dec saw something in the distance, nestled in the curve of a low hill.

What was it?

He brought the binoculars to his eyes.

The people who lived here were poor. The size of the farmhouses reflected that, but what he saw through the glasses was small even by local standards.

Was it a shed for animals? No. It wasn't big enough for that. Besides, if it housed living creatures, there'd have been a house nearby.

Some sheep farmers, those with large herds, drove their animals here for summer grazing. Maybe this was where a shepherd would spend those months.

Whatever it was, the little house seemed uninhabited.

Well, there was only one way to find out.

Annie, who had been drowsing against his back, jerked upright as he clucked softly to the horse and changed their direction.

"What's wrong?"

"There's a house by that hill." He handed the binoculars to her. "See it? All the way over there?"

"It's tiny."

"Yeah. It looks empty. Maybe it's a shepherd's summer camp. I'm hoping it is."

They approached the house slowly. When they got closer, his sense that nobody lived in it grow stronger.

No smoke came from the chimney; weeds and grass grew tall around its perimeter and at the door.

Still, he was cautious. Experience had taught him that it was always best to check things as much as you could rather than stumbling into them.

He drew the horse to a halt. Annie slid from the saddle. So did Dec, but when he held out the reins, she put her hands behind her back.

"If you're going in, so am I."

"Annie," he said patiently, "we aren't going to argue over this."

"You're right. We won't argue. I'm going with you and that's that."

His princess was a weary, scruffy mess, but her tone was imperious. Despite himself, he grinned, reached for her and drew her to him

"That's that? Like, you're setting the rules now?"

She put her palms against his chest. "Like, we're in this together. From now on, it's a fifty-fifty deal."

Dec tilted her head up. "A fifty-fifty deal, huh? What makes you think I'll agree to that?"

"You'll agree because you're a sensible man." Annie rose to him and kissed him. "And you know I'm right. Two of us should make this approach, Declan, not one."

Dec sighed. She was right, but he wasn't about to risk her life.

"Honey. The thing is, the place looks deserted—but someone might be inside. I don't want to take any chances."

"Neither do I." She stepped back and held out her

hand. "Which is why you're going to give me that Glock." When he didn't answer, she shook her head with impatience. "I didn't shoot myself in the foot with it last night, did I? Stop being so macho-stubborn and give me the gun!"

Macho-stubborn? Him? He wasn't...But it was true that even as upset as she'd been last night, she'd handled the Glock with the respect the weapon deserved.

Dec sighed, took the gun from its holster, checked that the safety was on and handed it to her.

"Okay," he said briskly. "Stay behind me. And that's not up for discussion. Stay behind me, or stay behind. You got that?"

Annie nodded. "Aye aye, Lieutenant."

Dec flashed a quick smile. "I like that attitude, Princess. Hang onto it until later."

She smiled back at him. Then his expression changed; he shifted his automatic rifle from his shoulder and cradled it in his arms as he crouched and began angling towards the house.

Annie fell in behind him.

She knew his method of approach was to keep them from being easy targets. And she did know some-thing about guns. Her father had taken her target shooting.

"A woman should be able to do anything a man can do," he'd said.

She wondered what her father would say if he could see her now. That she was running for her life would surely have broken his heart, but she hoped he would be proud of her for being strong.

What she knew was that her strength came from Declan.

Anything might happen in the next few minutes and though she could feel her heart hammering in her chest, she wasn't afraid.

Her courage had been slipping away until he'd found her. No. Not her courage, exactly. What she'd been losing had been the will to go on. Declan had changed that. He'd reminded her that there was still a reason to hope.

She would not give that up again.

When they were almost at the house. Declan held up his hand.

"Wait here," he said softly. "No arguing this time, or it could cost us our lives. Understood?"

"Understood," she whispered.

She watched as he crossed the last few feet. There was one window set in the front wall. When he reached it, he straightened up just enough to peer through it. Then he slid around the corner. She knew he was searching for other windows, other doors, and she waited for what seemed forever until the front door opened and revealed Declan, who flashed her a thumb's up.

"Two doors," he said as she hurried towards him, "one in front, one in back, and wait until you see the rest. All the comforts of home."

〜

HE WAS RIGHT.

Compared to a cave, this little house was—it made her smile to think it—a palace.

Sheepskin rugs on the floor. A bed. A big fireplace and a stack of firewood. A camping stove, a camping lantern, a big tin of kerosene—and three shelves filled with cans and cartons of food.

Annie clapped her hands with delight. "What more could we ask for?"

"An outhouse," Declan said. "A well. A lean-to for the horse complete with a couple of sacks of feed and a watering trough. And guess what? We have all that, right out back."

She gave an elaborate sigh. "Me first for the outhouse."

"You're sure you're okay with that? I checked. There's nothing living inside it, but it's not exactly paradise."

"I bet you think I've never used an outhouse before."

He looked up from the gear he was unpacking. "A buck says I'm right."

"Okay. I owe you a dollar—but an outhouse has to be better than squatting in the grass."

Declan tried not to laugh. "You are," he said solemnly, "what my old man would call a straight-talking woman."

"And you are," Annie said, just as solemnly, "what mine would have called a hero."

Dec's smile faded. "I'm no hero, honey. I'm just a soldier."

She went up to him, rose on her toes and kissed his cheek.

"A soldier would have put me on that helicopter. You didn't, even though you're probably going to face hell for that decision." She looked into his eyes. "I owe you some answers, Declan, and I'm going to give them to you."

Dec took her hands in his and brought them to his chest.

"First things first," he said quietly. "A hot meal. A hot drink. Maybe we'll even clean up a little." He touched his hand to her cheek and smiled. "Although I have to admit, I'm getting kind of fond of one or two of these dirt streaks."

She smiled back at him. She knew what he was doing—giving her time to get herself together, to work up to what he sensed was going to be a story as hard for her to tell as for him to hear.

"There are salons in Paris that would charge a fortune to paint streaks like these on my face. But you're right. We'll clean up, then open a couple of cans and boxes of whatever this stuff is." She rolled her eyes. "And I'm about to discover the charms of outdoor plumbing."

IT SEEMED that Declan was wrong.

There was something living in the outhouse—a spider that should have been wearing a collar and leash, but Annie figured as long as it kept to its side of an invisible line and she kept to hers, they could co-exist.

Just having the bare trappings of civilization energized her.

A little while ago, she'd been too tired to think.

Now, she felt renewed. Restored. Humming softly, she went back to the shepherd's cottage and shut the door behind her.

Declan had a fire going on the hearth, a huge bucket of water heating on the grate, and an big oval basin drawn up before it. He was crouched before the fire, tending it.

He was barefoot and shirtless, wearing only his camos.

The firelight played over him, illuminating his wide shoulders and muscled back.

There was a long scar low on his spine.

Annie felt a sudden sweet ache low in her belly.

She wanted to go to him and kiss the scar, kiss every part of him.

"Declan?" she said softly.

He rose to his feet and turned towards her. Her heart thudded. He was beautiful. His face was the essence of masculine strength and power. So was his body. Every part of him proclaimed him a proud warrior who had faced his enemies, fought them and won.

She realized she hadn't ever really seen him naked.

The light had been poor last night and though she'd felt every powerful inch of him against her, she'd learned the contours of his body mostly by touch.

She'd often slept in his arms in California, but he'd always kept on a T-shirt and board shorts. For her sake, she knew. And though he'd been shirtless on the beach, that didn't count.

They hadn't been lovers then.

Now they were, and she couldn't stop looking at him.

The muscled arms. The taut pectorals. The dog-tags glinting against the line of dark hair that traveled down his chest, over those washboard abs, to disappear into his camos.

His unbuttoned camos, riding low on his hips.

Her mouth went dry. Her gaze swept back to his face. He was watching her through narrowed eyes the color of night.

"Anoushka," he said, and for the first time since the deaths of her parents, her given name sounded as if it truly belonged to her. "I heated some water. I thought we might wash up before we eat."

She nodded. "Yes. Of course. Wash up..."

Slowly, he began walking towards her. He stopped only inches away. She could feel the heat of the fire, the heat of his body, the heat of desire burning inside her

"We should do a lot of things—but, baby, if I don't get inside you right now, I'm going to die."

His blunt words sent a shock of electricity racing from her breasts to her belly. In an instant, she was hot and wet, and when he reached for her, she threw herself into his arms, sobbing his name, eager for his kiss, his touch, his possession.

He thrust his hand into her hair and cupped the back of her head and then he took her mouth, not gently, not asking, he claimed her with his lips, his teeth, his tongue, and it was exactly what she wanted.

He bent down in front of her, unlaced her boots. She stepped out of them. Then he rose to his feet and tore her sweater over her head, undid her camo pants and shoved them and her panties to her ankles. His hands were hard and fast; so was his his breathing, and yes, this was how she wanted him, now, right now, no preliminaries, no gentle explorations, she wanted him to take her and make her fly.

"Jesus Christ," he said thickly. "Annie. Anoushka. I can't wait..."

He lifted her. Carried her to a narrow bed piled high with soft sheepskins. Tumbled onto it with her. She sobbed his name, reached up to him as he kicked off his pants and then he was inside her, deep inside her; her body lifted to his and her cry of immediate release was all he needed to let go and explode within her.

"Annie," he said, "Annie, I love you."

She wound her arms around him, drew him down against her, and wept with joy.

10

They stayed that way for a long, long time, Dec's arms hard around Annie, hers around him, hearts drumming against each other, then slowing, slowing, slowing until, gradually, reality returned.

Dec rolled to his side with Annie still in his arms. He kissed her throat. Softly. Tenderly. "You okay?"

She nodded. Some day, in some century, she would be able to form words—but not quite yet.

"I didn't mean to be so—"

She pressed a kiss to his mouth. She felt...Boneless. Breathless. And exhausted. So perfectly, happily exhausted...

"Hey." He nuzzled aside a strand of her hair and gently bit her shoulder. "No falling asleep, woman. First you need something to eat."

"Mmm."

"And all that water's gonna boil away to nothing."

She snuggled closer. "Mmm."

"If it does, I might just make you go out to the well to get more."

Annie gave a dramatic sigh. "You're a hard man, Sanchez."

Dec wiggled his eyebrows. "I certainly hope so."

She laughed. He smiled, kissed her again, and sat up. "Come on. We'll do a quick wash-up and then I'll make us my world-famous Chef's Special."

"Which is?" she said, letting him draw her up beside him.

"Which is whatever's in a couple of those boxes and cans. How's that sound?" Annie's stomach rumbled. Declan chuckled. "I couldn't have said it better myself."

He filled the basin by the fireplace with warm water. Then he led her to it. Annie stepped in and reached for a big bar of soap.

Dec took it from her.

"Lieutenant Sanchez at your service, my lady. Shampoo first?"

"Lovely," she sighed.

He washed her hair. Rinsed it. She almost purred with pleasure.

Next, he bathed her...Except there had to be a better word for what your lover did when he stroked you from head to toe with a soapy cloth, lingering in all the places only a lover would know.

"Not fair," she whispered, when he cupped her breasts and rolled her nipples between his fingers.

"Just trying to make sure I'm doing a good job," he said, but his husky voice gave him away.

And it really wasn't fair when he slipped his hand between her thighs and gently rubbed the wet cloth against her clitoris until her head fell back and she gave a soft, sweet moan.

"You just wait," she said. "I'm going to get even."

Dec looked down at his erect penis and gave a rueful laugh. "I hope so."

When it was her turn, she washed him with meticulous care, stroking the wet cloth over his face, his shoulders, his chest and back, pausing to kiss each scar.

She could feel the tension building in his muscles.

"Darn," she said.

"What?" His voice was low.

"I don't know how I missed this," she said with perfect innocence.

Her hand closed around his erection.

"Anoushka..."

She stroked him. He groaned and closed his eyes.

"Am I doing this right?" she whispered.

He put his hand over hers. "You're doing it right," he said hoarsely. "Just a little harder...That's it. That's..."

In one quick move, he was out of the basin, she was in his arms, and they were on the soft bed again.

"Anoushka," he growled, catching hold of her hands, tangling his fingers with hers, and when he thrust into her, she wrapped herself around him and her last thought, before her orgasm swept her away, was that this man, this moment, this joining of body and soul, was the very purpose of life.

∽

SHE CAME AWAKE SLOWLY, yawning, stretching, feeling warm and snug in a cocoon of soft wool blankets.

A wonderful aroma filled the air.

Something spicy. Cinnamon. Nutmeg. Apple...

"Hey."

She blinked and rolled onto her side.

Declan was squatting beside her. He had on a black T-shirt and shorts.

"Hey yourself," she murmured. "How long did I sleep?"

"Less than an hour."

"Mmm." She stretched again. "Feels longer than that." She wiggled her nose. "What's that amazing smell?"

"It's dinner, princess." He leaned in and gave her a tender kiss. "I washed our stuff and hung it to dry, and I have a clean shirt for you." A quick, sexy smile curved his lips. "Unless you'd rather go casual."

"Casual?"

"Uh huh." He kissed her again. "As in, clothing optional."

Annie laughed and sat up. "The clean shirt sounds good."

He sighed. "Difficult woman," he said, and handed her a shirt that was a twin of his.

She pulled it on and got to her feet. The shirt hung halfway down her thighs. No pants was casual enough. In fact, knowing she was naked beneath the shirt put a knot of warmth low in her belly. Her hair was still damp; she ran her fingers through it and let it settle against her shoulders.

She felt absolutely wonderful.

And Declan—Declan *was* wonderful. He'd not only washed their clothes, he'd made dinner and set the table with earthenware bowls, spoons, mugs, and in the center, a jug filled with what looked like pussy willows.

Annie sat in one of the two chairs. "Very nice."

Declan grinned as he lifted a big pot from the fireplace and brought it to the table. "Only the best for the Presidential Suite."

"Mmm. Smells good."

"Maine lobster always smells good." He laughed at the look on her face. "It's oatmeal with spices and brown sugar tossed in. Some dried apple slices too. We'll have to leave our anonymous host a thank you note along with the number of my credit card."

Annie looked at him. "Are you sure he won't, you know, drop in on us?"

Dec filled both bowls, then sat down across from her.

"Based on the dust, the super-clean hearth, I don't think anyone's used this place for months. It might be abandoned. Even if it isn't, nobody who's moving sheep up from a valley is going to do it for at least another few weeks. Go on, honey. Dig in."

She spooned up some of the oatmeal, put it in her mouth and sighed with pleasure.

"Declan Sanchez! You've been holding out on me. I never knew you could cook."

"Not true! Have you forgotten my beef empanadas? My General Tso's chicken? How about my specialty, pizza with garlic and pepperoni?"

She laughed. "You mean the takeout from the Mexican place, the Chinese place and the pizza place?"

"Details, details. Want some tea?"

"Tea would be wonderful."

Dec rose, got a small tin canister from a shelf, opened it, dumped tea leaves in their mugs and then added boiling water as Annie gave each of them another serving of oatmeal.

"My mother taught me to cook," she said. She laughed at the doubtful expression on his face. "Well, okay. Not really. She could only make one thing. Brownies. She'd learned how from a roommate when she was at school, and she made them for me a few times a year. They were a special treat."

"My mom's specialty was corn fritters. She'd tell me to bring in a couple of dozen ears of corn and I'd run out and pick those ears as fast as I could 'cause the faster I picked 'em and husked 'em, the faster those fritters got into my belly."

Annie smiled. "You grew up on a farm?"

"You could call it that, I guess." Dec drank some of his tea. "We had a few acres."

"But you didn't want to be a farmer."

"Me?" He smiled. "I wanted to be the quarterback for the Green Bay Packers. Or maybe pitch for the Red Sox. Somehow get to the UK and be drafted by Manchester United."

"A sports hero," she said, laughing.

"Uh huh. Only one drawback. I was good at sports, but not good enough to win a scholarship. And I knew I needed a degree if I was going to get out into the world."

"So you joined the Navy?"

He pushed his empty bowl away. "I had this thing about computers. Kind of a skill."

"I remember what you did for Chay and Bianca." Annie smiled. "Very impressive. I mean, I'm good at computers, but you..."

"I just have a feel for coding." He grinned. "Especially for hacking. Of course, I didn't mention the hacking part when I applied to bunch of colleges. NYU —New York University— offered me a scholarship, but after I graduated the idea of sitting at a desk for the rest of my life..." He shrugged. "Then I lucked out. I met this guy, a friend of a friend. He was a SEAL. He wouldn't talk much about his work, but the little he said...I knew it sounded right. So I asked him how to become a SEAL. A long time later, I realized I was lucky he hadn't laughed in my face..." Dec rolled his eyes. "Man, just listen to me! You've got me babbling."

Annie reached for his hand. "I want to know everything about you, Declan. Everything! Your favorite color. Your favorite book. What you were like as a little boy..." She hesitated. "But right now—now, I guess it's time for me to tell you about me."

Her voice was low; her face, when she lifted it and looked at him, wore an expression that made his throat tighten.

Dec knew she was about to tell him what he

needed to hear, what they'd both done a good job of avoiding, and suddenly he thought, to hell with putting her through this. He knew the bad guys who were after them—her uncle, her would-be bridegroom, the bastards who'd kidnapped her, the terrorist who wanted her, and what did it matter if he knew how all of them came together?

He didn't even have to know why she'd left him.

Not anymore. She was his. That was all that mattered—although yeah, some day he'd want the whole story so he could deal with the uncle, the groom, the kidnappers, the so-called Deliverer, but the bottom line was that getting her home had nothing to do with any of that.

"Annie," he said, "you know what? You don't have to do this. I believe everything you told me about your uncle, and I'm sure you had a good reason for leaving me, and—"

"I have to talk about it." She laced her fingers through his and drew a long, deep breath. "Because here's the most important thing. I didn't leave you. I mean, I knew I had to—it was why I'd started to see you less often—but I couldn't bring myself to make the break." Her eyes filled with tears; she brought their joined hands to her face and pressed kisses to his knuckles. "I loved you. I loved you. I would never have—"

"Anoushka." Declan pushed back his chair, reached for her and drew her into his lap. "Don't cry, baby. Please. Don't cry. Remember what I said? If you can't talk about it—"

She put her fingers lightly over his mouth, took another deep breath, and began with her childhood in Qaram.

"I was always happy. Nobody's always happy, but I really was. My parents loved me and I adored them. " She smiled. "I have lots of wonderful memories. Seeing mountain gorillas in Rwanda. Going to the top of the Eiffel Tower. A trip to Disneyland." Declan raised his eyebrows and she gave a soft laugh. "I had my picture taken with Minnie Mouse."

Dec smiled and gathered her closer. "Not Mickey?"

"I thought Minnie had been overlooked. She was a girl mouse, but that didn't make her less important than Mickey."

Dec laughed. "A feminist at, what, age ten?"

"Seven," Annie said, laughing with him, "but that's how I was raised." Her expression grew serious. "My parents wanted changes in Qaram. The country was eager to embrace technology, but it was difficult to move cultural attitudes forward. That was part of the reason I decided to take a graduate degree in computer studies. I'd already studied engineering. Coding seemed a good next step."

Dec gave a soft whistle. "I'm impressed."

"So was my uncle." A muscle in her jaw tightened. "Although that's not the right way to put it. He thought my parents were making a terrible mistake. As far as he was concerned, the old ways were sacrosanct. No education for girls beyond what Americans would call the eighth grade. No women in the professions. He and my father argued over my father's plans for Qaram and over my plans for my future. "

"But your father was king."

Annie nodded. "And he was determined. He established an advisory governing council. At first they rubber-stamped whatever he said, but he worked hard and with the support of a trusted appointee to that council, the members began to speak up, to offer opinions of their own." She paused. "And then—and then, my father and mother died in a plane crash."

Her voice wobbled.

Dec drew her head to his shoulder. He rocked her gently in his arms., felt her hot tears on his neck.

"Anoushka. If it hurts too much to talk about this—"

She sat up straight and wiped her hands over her eyes. "They died, and the council member who was my father's oldest friend warned me not to come home. He said—he said it was possible my parents had been murdered, and that he feared for my life if I returned to Qaram, even for the funeral. I'd registered at school as Annie Stanton to avoid publicity. He told me to truly become Annie Stanton and forget I'd ever been a woman named Anoushka."

Another steadying breath, and then she told Declan everything.

How she'd had to mourn the awful loss of her parents alone.

How she'd lived in fear of being found.

How she'd resigned herself to despair and solitude.

"And then I met you," she said softly, "and everything changed."

Declan cupped the back of her head and brought his mouth to hers.

"You were all I'd ever dreamed of," Annie whispered. "Strong. Tender. You cared about people, about your friends..." She smiled and put her hand against his cheek. "You cared about me."

Dec turned his face into her hand and kissed her palm.

"I think I fell in love with you that first day on the beach," he said. "I'd never known a woman like you. Sweet and beautiful, kind and generous... " He returned her smile. "And smart. So smart you scared me."

Annie laughed. "It was the same for me. I thought, how did I get so lucky?" Her smile tilted. "Declan? I knew you wanted more. Sex, I mean."

"Honey. You were so innocent. I wanted you—but I couldn't bring myself to rush you." His mouth twisted. "It never occurred to me that remaining a virgin was part of your—"

"That wasn't why I never slept with you, Declan." She swallowed hard. "I wanted to. I wanted to, desperately. But you were so good, so honest—and all the time, I was lying to you. Maybe it sounds crazy, but the thought of giving myself to you without also telling you the truth about me seemed—it seemed obscene." Annie paused. "That was when I realized I had to break thing off between us."

"What I don't get is why you didn't confide in me.

Didn't you trust me enough to tell me who you were and what had happened to you?"

She gave another of those soft, sad laughs.

"I trusted you with all my heart—and that was the problem. By then, my uncle had taken over Qaram. In the blink of an eye, our two countries had become alienated. You're a warrior, Declan. A man of honor and duty. I'm the niece—the titled niece—of a man well on his way to becoming your country's enemy. I knew you wouldn't hide that from your superior officers, that you'd tell them about our relationship, And then what? Would they still let you serve your country or would they see that as the end to your career? And if it was—if it was, how could you possibly go on caring for me?"

Declan gathered her hard against him. He held her for long moments, loving the feel of her in his arms, loving her courage—and knowing she was right. Once his superiors knew about her, it probably would have meant his career in Special Ops—in the military—was over.

She'd sacrificed herself for him rather than let him sacrifice himself for her, because he would have given up everything to be with her.

That was how it was when you loved a woman the way he loved his Annie.

And—and—

A knot formed in his belly.

All at once, he knew, goddammit, he *knew* that even though she'd decided to end their relationship she'd never have left him without a word. A note. Something. She wouldn't have just vanished from his life. She was too decent, too giving.

How come he'd never considered that before?

"Annie," he said, trying to sound as if he wasn't already feeling anger building in his blood, "you didn't just leave Santa Barbara, did you?"

She looked away from him.

This was the one part she wished she could keep secret. Bad enough she'd told him her uncle had kept her prisoner and sold her to the King of Tharsalonia. The rest would enrage him, and she knew enough about STUD warriors to know that her Declan would want to avenge her.

"Annie." Declan turned her on his lap so that she was straddling him. His eyes bored into hers. "Tell me exactly what happened."

So she did.

She told about waking in the middle of the night to find two men in her bedroom. Told him about the threats they'd made to hurt someone she cared about.

"Someone you cared about. " Dec's tone was ominously calm. "Was I that someone?"

Annie looked away from him. Deb grabbed her chin and forced her to meet his eyes.

" I did what I had to do," she whispered.

"I could have handled them," he said calmly. Much too calmly. "And then?"

"They had a car waiting. A black SUV with tinted windows and diplomatic plates." Annie ran the tip of her tongue over her lips. "They took me to the airport. To a part I'd never seen before."

"The area reserved for private planes."

"Yes. They put me on a plane and we flew to Qaram."

"And when you got there?"

Once again, she tried to turn her face away. Dec wouldn't let her.

"Tell me the rest."

His touch was gentle. His voice was steady. But his eyes were flat; his breathing was swift. She could almost feel his body humming with rage.

"My uncle confined me to my rooms. Not all the time. If he had guests—important guests—he expected me to join him." Her mouth trembled. "But I refused. No matter how angry he got, how much he threatened, I wouldn't do it. It made him furious. He said I was a drain on the kingdom and he promised he'd find some way to make me useful."

Dec nodded. His Annie. His Anoushka. His brave, honorable princess who had given up everything for him...

"And this marriage would make you useful."

"Yes. He's planning to invade the kingdom of Suwaith. It's a small country—"

"—on Qaram's southern border," Dec said grimly. "One of our allies, rich in oil and minerals."

"Yes. And Suwaith is—it *was* an ally of Tharsalonia. So my my uncle made a deal with the Tharsalonian king. He'd give him several million dollars to turn a blind eye to the planned invasion." She hesitated. "And he'd give him me."

"And you told your uncle you wouldn't agree."

She shuddered. "I told him I would never—that I would never..." Her voice hardened. "It's why I told you not to worry about us making love without a condom. My uncle sent me to—to be examined. To be sure I was a virgin. Otherwise, my bridal price would not have been high enough."

Declan said nothing. How could he, when he was so filled with fury?

"The doctor who examined me had been a friend of my mother's." Annie's tone softened. "She said she would assure my uncle that I was a virgin—but she knew I was unhappy. I cried, you know? I couldn't help it. I cried when she asked me how I felt about the marriage. About—about bearing the king's children."

"She gave you birth control pills," Dec said softly.

"Not pills. She gave me a shot. Someone could have seen me taking pills. The shot lasts for three months. She warned me that after that—that after that—"

Dec used his fingertips to wipe away Annie's tears. "She's a good woman."

Annie nodded. She sat quietly in his arms, her head resting against his shoulder. After a few minutes, Dec put his fingers under her chin and raised her face to his.

"I failed you," he said in a harsh voice.

"You? Never! You could never—"

"After you hadn't phoned for a few days, after you hadn't taken my calls, I went to your apartment."

She smiled. "My shoebox-size rented rooms, you mean."

"I used the key you'd given me to get in. And you

were gone. I mean, everything that you were was gone. Your clothes. Your books. The sea shells you used to pick up on the beach..."

Her smile tilted. "The men who came for me said they would see to removing all my things."

Dec leaned his forehead against hers.

"Your landlord said you'd decided to move. That you'd left no forwarding address."

"Yes. The men who took me—"

"How could I have believed him? You'd never have done something like that. Even if you'd decided to end things between us, you'd have told me." His voice roughened. "My pride. My ego. Whatever you call it, I let it take over when what I should have done was go looking for you."

"And you would have, if only I'd told you the truth."

He drew her to him. She buried her face against his shoulder.

"Those bastards," he said softly. "Your uncle. And Amjad."

Annie pulled back. "Declan. Promise me you won't do anything foolish."

His lips drew back from his teeth in a wolfish smile. "I won't do anything foolish."

"I mean it. My uncle has no scruples. And Amjad..." She framed his face with her hands. "Please, my love, please, promise me you won't do anything foolish."

It was the first time she had called him her love.

The words sang in his blood, in his heart, but there was no stopping the rage that coursed through him.

"Declan?"

Dec switched off the lantern, then brushed his lips over Annie's and rose to his feet with her in his arms.

"I promise," he said. "I won't do anything foolish."

He carried her to their bed and lay down with her, wrapping them both in a soft woolen blanket, holding her close as her breathing slowed into the steady rhythm of sleep.

A muscle ticked in his jaw. He'd made her a promise and he would keep it.

There was nothing even remotely foolish about eliminating the uncle and the terrorist who had chosen to sentence his Annie to what would have been a life of slavery.

11

The soft patter of rain woke Dec in the middle of the night.

He'd already left the warmth of the bed and the warmth of the woman he loved so he could slip outside to make sure the perimeter was still secure.

Time to check again.

He'd done what he could to secure the house. He'd emptied out a couple of soup cans, punched holes in the tops, half-filled them with pebbles and strung the cans on paracord. Then he'd tied the cord to trees and shrubs to make a kind of barrier around the house. He'd also rigged lines at the doors and at the single window.

At least an intruder would not be able to make a quiet approach.

Now, he pressed a light kiss to Annie's hair, rose from the bed, pulled on his almost-dry camo pants, undid the alarm system at the back door and eased outside.

He was greeted by familiar night sounds. Always a good sign. He took a quick look into the lean-to. The horse had his head down and was asleep.

Nothing had been disturbed.

Dec was more and more certain that the men following them had gone west instead of north. Tomorrow, he'd give the satphone another try. If it worked, he'd arrange for a rendezvous. If it didn't, he'd have to wait until they reached the market town at the border and hope somebody there would have a telephone.

One way or another, he'd get Annie to safety. To Santa Barbara and his cottage. Their cottage. From now on, it would belong to them both. Once he did, he'd find a way to come back and deal with her uncle Cyrus and with Altair Amjad..

He entered the cottage soundlessly, re-rigged the warning system, took off his pants and rubbed down with a towel. Then he returned to the narrow bed.

In his absence, Annie had moved into the center of it. There was just space enough for him to climb onto the mattress and wrap one arm around her.

She sighed and rolled onto her side. Shifted her sweet ass so it pressed into the cradle of his thighs.

A gentleman would have moved back a couple of inches and if that wasn't possible, a gentleman would have grabbed a sheepskin and made himself a bed on the floor.

But Dec wasn't a gentleman, not when it came to how he reacted to his woman. His body responded instantly, sending his blood straight to his dick.

Forget it, he told himself. She needed sleep.

His hand moved from her hip to her waist to her breast.

He closed his eyes, savoring the feel of it, the way the nipple kissed his palm.

He bit back a groan. Told himself what a no-good bastard he was even to think about having her again...

Too bad his dick didn't get the message.

The head of it was seeking comfort, seeking Annie's heat.

And, God, she was hot. Wet. Her body was ready to welcome his.

He moved.

Just a little.

Half an inch.

A little more

She sighed. "Declan," she whispered sleepily.

She reached back, put her hand between them, stroked him.

He slipped inside her. Slowly. Slowly.

She said his name again and he slid deeper into her silky softness. She moaned.

"Baby," he said thickly, rocking against her.

"Yes," she said, "yes yes, like that. Like that. Like..."

Her muscles convulsed around him; she threw her head back and cried out into the night.

He came with her, sinking his teeth lightly into her shoulder as he did.

They stayed that way for long minutes. Then he turned her towards him.

"Never leave me again," he said gruffly.

She clasped his face between her hands. "Never. Never, never, never!"

He kissed her. And then he was hard again, he needed her again, and he rolled her onto her back and she wrapped her legs around his hips and took him into her.

He rode her, hard and fast.

They came together, flying through the night with the swift brilliance of shooting stars.

They they tumbled into sleep.

THE NEXT TIME DEC WOKE, it was dawn. He'd rigged a blanket over the window, but the early morning light managed to slip through the soft weave.

He lay on his back, his arms around Annie who lay half-sprawled over him. They must have been lying that way for a couple of hours because his muscles felt a little stiff, but he wouldn't have moved for anything in the world.

He loved the feel of her against him, the whisper of her breath on his throat, the silky drift of her hair against his chest.

He stroked her hair. Her back. She sighed and rolled onto her side. He rose up on one elbow. Her lips were slightly parted and he gave into temptation, bent his head and kissed her.

Even in sleep, her mouth clung softly to his.

God, he loved her!

He knew now that he'd always loved her; he just

hadn't been ready to admit it to himself. Love—the forever kind of love—was scary as shit when you'd lived strictly for yourself for such a long time. Not that he'd never loved anybody. He loved his parents. His STUD brothers. But the one man, one woman thing?

He'd never thought about it much and when he had, he'd been unable to imagine wanting only one woman for the rest of his life.

Dec took a strand of Annie's dark hair and let it run through his fingers.

Now he couldn't imagine wanting anyone else.

It still killed him that he'd let himself believe she'd just packed up and left him. Sure, he'd felt her putting up a wall between them, but he should have known she'd never have walked away without some sort of explanation.

He'd been so fucking focused on himself that he'd been blind to everything else. Even at the wedding, during those few moments he'd been alone with her, he should have known something was wrong. She'd had a sad look in her eyes, a sorrow that was almost palpable, but instead of asking her about that he'd asked why she hadn't told him she was a princess.

Because you never asked, she'd replied.

Jesus.

Such a dumb question, and such an empty answer. Or maybe not. Maybe she'd meant he'd never asked her the things he should have. Even that day, he'd walked away instead of saying *Why did you leave me? Why did you run away when you must have known that I loved you?*

But she hadn't known, because he hadn't told her.

Well, he was going to make up for that omission. He was going to tell her he loved her every day for the rest of their lives. That she completed him. That she was everything he could ever want.

Pathetic male creature that he was, he wanted her now.

Okay. It was time to get away from temptation. She had to be tired. Maybe sore from all the times they'd made love. He had to leave her alone. Get up. See about making some coffee. Check the shelves for breakfast stuff. Crackers. Jam. Was there such a thing as peanut butter in this part of the world?

In other words, do something useful instead of lying here and imagining making love to her.

Dec began to ease away, but Annie gave a little hum of protest and flung her arm over his chest.

He held still. Seconds went by.

He tried again.

Another murmur of protest—and this time, she tossed her leg over his.

Oh, man.

Dec gritted his teeth.

Her leg was high over his. High enough so she was open against him. He could feel her heat, her dampness on his skin.

His dick shot to immediate attention.

He shut his eyes. Silently began counting. One. Two. Three...

"Good morning."

Her voice was soft and sexy. And her hand...Ah,

dear God. Her hand was snaking down his chest, down his belly...

"You're asking for trouble, Princess," he growled.

She laughed. It was a deep, dirty, wonderful laugh. "I certainly hope so, Lieutenant."

"Anoushka." Her hand closed around him. Sweat beaded his forehead. "Honey. You must be sore."

She was. Riding behind him on the horse had put a strain on her thighs. And they'd made love so many, many times...

Still, there was no way she could get enough of him. Her Declan. Her lover. A little soreness was a small price to pay for the joy of having him inside her.

She told him that, not with words, with her body. She moved over him, kissed him, and he groaned, clasped her hips and brought her down on his erect penis.

She moaned. Her head fell back. She raised herself and slowly came down on him again.

"Is that good?" she whispered.

Dec gave a tortured laugh. "It's perfect."

He put his hand between them, found her clit, caressed it while she slid up and down his hard length.

He was never going to get enough of this. Of her. He would never lose her again. Never. So what if he was a soldier? So what if she was a princess? So what if their two nations were enemies...

"Declan," Annie whispered.

There were tears in her eyes. His heart clenched.

"Sweetheart. Am I hurting you?"

"No. Oh no, Declan. I just—I love you. I love you. I love—"

"Anoushka," he said, and he stopped thinking, tumbled her beneath him, and swept reality away.

THEY FOUND COFFEE, sugar, even a small can of condensed milk. A box of something Dec swore looked like small brown floor tiles, and a jar of something that turned out to be jam.

"A feast," Annie said, laughing.

Dec poured some of the condensed milk into his coffee, took a sip and rolled his eyes.

"Heaven."

"The coffee?"

"Well, sure. But mostly the condensed milk, that combo of sugar and cream...My mom used to bake Christmas cookies and one of the ingredients was condensed milk. I loved it."

"The cookies or the milk?"

Dec grinned. "Both."

Annie reached for the can and read the label.

"I bet you can get a sugar-high from this stuff," she said.

She dipped her finger into the can and raised the finger to her lips, but Dec grabbed her hand and sucked her finger into the heat of his mouth.

"Super delicious," he said. "And you're the best sugar-high I can think of."

She smiled, leaned towards him and rested her head on his shoulder.

"So your mom baked cookies?"

"Yeah. Well, when she had the time. She drove to work in Taos every day. It was thirty miles one way. Plus there was always a lot to do around our place."

"That field of corn."

He smiled. "Right. And we had a big vegetable garden. We kept chickens. And we had a couple of horses."

"What did your mother do in Taos?"

Declan looked at Annie.

"She cleaned houses," he said. "And motel rooms. Not any more, though." He cleared his throat. "I've been, you know, I've been able to help out a little."

Annie nodded. Of course he helped out. She'd never met anyone with a bigger heart than her Declan.

"And your father? What about him?"

"My old man's a great guy. He paints. He sculpts. Last time I was home, he'd taken up pottery. "

"An artist," Annie said with delight.

"Only problem is, he's not very good at the commercial end of it. I don't think he's sold more than a dozen pieces of his work in a decade." Dec took her hand and played with her fingers. "Sounds like the setup for a five-handkerchief boy-girl movie. My mother cleaned houses and my dad's a dreamer. Your mother was a debutante and your and father ruled a kingdom."

"Declan. You're not going to tell me you think that matters!"

He kissed each of her fingertips.

"I'm not going to tell you that, no—but you have to admit, it's a little unusual."

"You're what's unusual," she said softly.

"No way, honey. That title belongs to you."

She smiled at him. He smiled back, leaned in, brushed his lips over hers and felt a sudden, overwhelming sense of foreboding.

They kept talking about being together, but how was that going to work? The cards were stacked against them. Yes, absolutely, she would not return to Qaram. And yes, absolutely, he would find a way to deal with the men who had harmed her. But it was hard enough to find happy endings in today's world even when there were no obvious barriers in the way...

"Whatever you're thinking," Annie said, "stop thinking it."

Annie's arms were folded over her chest. Her eyes were narrowed. She was all determination and intensity.

He laughed and pulled her into his lap.

"Kiss me," he said, "and then get that lovely ass in gear because we have work to do."

She gave him the kind of smile that would have melted iron. "Is that what you think? That I have a lovely ass?"

He grinned and set her on her feet.

"I'll answer that question later—but only if you've been a very, very good girl."

"How good?" she said, batting her lashes.

Dec nipped the side of her throat. "Extremely

good," he said in a sexy whisper. Then he slapped her lightly on her backside and they got to work, straightening things up and packing their gear.

ANNIE HAD HOPED to find a curry comb in the lean-to, but none turned up so she used a couple of rough rags to rub down the horse.

The horse didn't have any objections. In fact, after a few minutes, he snorted, lowered his big head and rubbed it against hers.

She paused and stroked his neck. "I agree," she whispered. "It's time for a break. I don't know why, but my head's starting to hurt."

"What's hurting?"

Annie turned around. "Declan." She smiled. "I thought Big Boy here could do with a little TLC."

"What did you way about something hurting?"

"Nothing." She sighed when Dec raised his eyebrows. "I have a little headache. Don't look at me like that. It's nothing."

"I have some ibuprofen in my gear."

"I don't need ibuprofen. Really. I'm..." Her gave went to the satphone in his hand and her smile faded. If the phone worked, that would be the good news and the bad news. They had been so happy here...

"The phone. Does it work now?"

"We're about to find out." He sat down on a wooden bench by the door and gestured to her to come sit next to him. Once she had, he activated the phone.

A click. A hum. And Dec heard the voice of the Recovery Mission COM OP in his ear.

"Lieutenant Sanchez? Jesus. I mean, heck, sir, is that you?"

"Who is this?"

"Billy Taylor, sir. Ensign William B. Taylor. Sir."

"Taylor. Can the 'sir' crap and put me through to Captain Black."

"Yessir. I mean, jeez, sir, we've been goin' nuts here, wondering what happened to you and the lady. I mean—"

"Goddammit, Taylor. Put me –"

"Sanchez?"

Dec let out his breath. "Captain."

"You okay?"

"Fine, sir."

"And the princess?"

Dec reached for Annie's hand. "She's fine too, sir."

"What the fuck happened? Why didn't you make it to the bird?"

Okay. So his guys hadn't said he and Annie could have made it, only that they hadn't. He owed them— but then, that was what SEALS and STUDs were all about. They had the loyalty of brothers to each other.

"Sanchez? You hear the question?"

"Yessir. We didn't make it to the Black Hawk because it wasn't safe for the princess." *True enough.* "I'll explain more when I see you."

"Yes. You will." A tiny pause before Black spoke again. "Right now, we need to get you evacuated. We've been trying to raise you for almost three days—we had some kind of satellite failure...Hang on, Sanchez. We're picking up your coordinates."

"Good to hear, sir. We need to get out ASAP."

"I'll contact you again in three minutes."

The line went dead. Dec glanced at his watch as he shut off the phone. Annie squeezed his hand.

"What did he say?"

"They're figuring out exactly where we are and where to extract us."

"Oh."

It was a very subdued *oh*. Dec put his thumb under her chin and gently tilted her face up to his.

"Anoushka. We're going to be fine."

She gave him a little smile. "I'm glad we're going to get out of here. The thing is, I know this is going to sound crazy, but—"

"These last days have been wonderful."

She nodded. "Yes. Despite everything, they've been —they've been the best days of my life."

Dec leaned in and kissed her. "Mine too. But this is only the beginning, honey. We have years and years ahead of us."

"Yes."

The word was barely a whisper. Dec drew Annie close.

"We do, sweetheart. You'll see. I know we have a lot to work out." *Man, talk about understatements...* "But we'll do it. I know we will."

She nodded again. "Just don't let them send me back, Declan. Because if they do..."

The phone buzzed. Dec pushed a button and put it to his ear.

"Sanchez," he said crisply.

"Lieutenant. Do you have your GPS?"

"No sir. It's gone."

"But you have a map."

"Yessir."

"Okay, then," Black said. "Here's the deal."

The CO rattled off time, map coordinates, a mountain to cross and, on the other side of that mountain, a stretch of empty beach where they'd be picked up.

"Got that, Sanchez?"

Dec nodded. "Got it, sir. One more mountain, then a beach, then extraction."

"Yeah. I wish we could get you out without sending you up that mountain, but you're on disputed turf. Bad enough, but sending in a couple of heavily armed birds —Washington says no."

"Understood."

"Also, weatherman says you're in for high winds later today. Maintain a steady pace, you should be over the mountain by then."

"Sounds good, Captain."

"Sanchez. You have an interesting assortment of motherfuckers who'd like to get their hands on you."

"Yessir."

"Intel says you've done a good job of losing most of them."

"Good to hear."

"Altair Amjad's the one you'll have to watch out for.

He's smart, he's hot on your trail, and he wants what you have."

Damn right he did. He wanted Annie.

"In other words, he's pissed off, Sanchez. You are not his favorite person."

Dec knew exactly what that meant. No way could the terrorist survive the humiliation of being outfoxed by one STUD operative, especially when it had cost him his very special prize.

"Sir," Declan said. "About the princess..."

"Yes?"

"I have information you don't have."

"It can wait."

"Captain. You should hear this now."

"Sanchez. There's no way of knowing what the enemy might be picking up. And if you want to make it to the extraction point on time..."

"Yessir. I understand. But you need to know that the princess does not want to return to Qaram." Annie took his hand and squeezed it. "She *must* not return to Qaram, sir. The situation there is not what we were lead to believe."

"I hear you."

Annie squeezed his hand again. Dec nodded. "Captain. She can't be sent back."

"I got it the first time, unless you think I have a hearing problem."

"No sir. I'm just trying to clarify—"

"Clarify getting your ass out of there," Black said brusquely. "Understood?"

"Understood, sir."

"Remember your duty, Lieutenant."

The satphone went silent. Dec thought about Black's last comment. What the hell was that all about? When had he ever not remembered his duty?

"Declan?"

"Yeah." Dec frowned. She looked pale. "Sweet-heart? Are you okay?"

"I'm fine. It's just this headache..."

"I want you to take some ibuprofen."

"If I need it, I'll let you know."

"Stubborn woman," Dec said, smiling. He reached for her hand. "The headache's my fault. You needed to rest, and I haven't given you time to do that."

She brought their joined hands to her lips. "You've given me exactly what I needed," she said softly. "You."

"Soon," he said, leaning in for a quick kiss, "we'll have all the time in the world for each other."

She nodded. Hesitated. Sank her teeth lightly into her bottom lip.

"Declan? That was your commanding officer, right?"

"Uh huh. Jim Black. You met him at the Landing Zone. That party for Chay and Bianca, remember? He's getting us out of here. A few more hours and this will all be history."

Annie smiled again, but this time the smile didn't quite reach her eyes.

"And he won't send me back to Qaram."

"Honey. You heard what I told him. No. He won't send you back."

"Sorry. I'm being foolish."

"You're being cautious. And who could blame you for that?" Dec caught a strand of her hair and tucked it behind her ear. "Anoushka. I let you go once and I'm never going to make that mistake again. You're mine, and I'm yours, and nothing can change that."

She went into his arms. They kissed and held each other tight.

"You're right," she said softly. "I'm yours—and no matter what happens, that will never change."

THEY CLEANED up whatever they'd disturbed in the sheepherder's cottage. When they were done, Dec took some bills from his pocket and put them on the table.

"Local currency?" Annie said in surprise.

"Carrying some is standard Special Ops practice. You never know what you might need if things go wrong." He saw the sudden darkness in Annie's eyes. "But nothing's going to go wrong for us," he said quickly. "We're too close to the end."

The truth was, a dozen things could go wrong, straight up to the last second, but why borrow trouble ahead of time?

"Okay," he said briskly. "Time to go. Too bad the guy who owns this place isn't here. I'd probably kiss him."

Annie laughed.

That was good.

He'd wanted to make her laugh. There was still a

hint of darkness in her eyes, as if she were looking ahead and seeing something she didn't want to see.

Okay. He'd replace that something with a better image.

"Know what I'm thinking of?" he said, drawing her into his arms.

She leaned back in his embrace and smiled up at him. "A hot shower? A porterhouse steak? A king size bed?"

He grinned. "Sounds excellent. And in exactly that order—but that's not what I was thinking."

"No?"

"No." He waggled his eyebrows. "I'm thinking about what you're going to be wearing tomorrow. Well, okay. The day after tomorrow, when we're sitting on the beach in Santa Barbara."

"The day after tomorrow." She smiled. "And you're thinking about bathing suits?"

"Of course. It's a logical progression."

Another laugh, soft and sweet. "What kind would you like me to wear?"

"Well, I've always been a bikini man, but that black one piece number you wore a lot was actually kinda sexy."

"The black swimsuit it is." She touched her finger to his jaw. "Or I'll buy a bikini. My very first. Your choice."

Dec sucked her finger into the warmth of his mouth. "How about nothing?"

"Nothing, what?" It took a couple of seconds. "You mean, no suit at all?"

"Just you," he said. "Naked. All silky skin and nothing else."

His words, the huskiness in his voice, sent a wave of liquid longing straight through her.

"Mmm." She rose on her toes, her palms flat against his chest,, and brushed her lips over his. "You're a creative man, Lieutenant."

"You ain't seen nothin' yet," he said, and kissed her.

But when the kiss ended, so did the teasing. Dec cupped Annie's face and looked straight into her eyes.

"We're going to be fine," he said. "We're going to get out of here. And then we're going to spend the rest of our lives together."

12

Dec checked his map.

The walk to the rendezvous point wasn't going to be easy.

They'd have to leave the dirt road, angle across the increasingly arid plateau, then scale the mountain Black had told him about. All that, plus they had a tight deadline to meet, but it was doable.

All they had to do was get started and keep moving.

"Okay," he said. "We have a tough few miles ahead of us, but...Honey?"

Annie was sitting on the edge of the bed. She looked...She looked wrong.

"Annie. What's the matter?"

"Nothing."

No way was he buying that. Dec knelt beside her. "The truth," he said, "What's going on?"

"I'm just kind of achy."

"Your head?"

"My head. My neck." She tried for a smile and didn't quite make it. "It's nothing. Really. I'm fine."

She didn't look fine. Her eyes were too bright; her face was flushed. Dec felt her forehead. She didn't seem to be running a fever, but he couldn't be positive.

He rose to his feet and brought her a cup of water. She took it and he saw her hands shake when she lifted it to her lips.

He got the ibuprofen from his pack and held out three tablets.

"Really, I'm..." She rolled her eyes at the look on his face. With a sigh of resignation, she took the tablets, swallowed them down with another gulp of water.

Dec sat down put his arm around her shoulders. She leaned against him.

"I don't want to delay us."

"You won't. Just give the tablets a couple of minutes to do their job. Okay?"

"Okay," she said, with a quick smile.

He smoothed his hand over her hair. He'd factored a lot of things into getting her to safety. Time was becoming the most important one. If she was sick, if he couldn't get her to the extraction site...

No. He wasn't going to think that way.

She was tired. Her muscles were protesting all the walking and climbing and riding. All the sex. The ibuprofen would kick in and she'd be fine. He just had to help keep it together until he got her to the extraction point.

Minutes slipped past.

Annie showed no sign of moving. Dec checked his

watch. Unless they got started soon, they'd be late for their pickup.

"Honey? We have some travelling ahead of us. We can rest after that."

"Of course." She stood up. "See? I'm fine. The ibuprofen did the trick."

He didn't think so. She was wobbly, and she still didn't look right, but what choice did they have?

He mounted the horse, got Annie up behind him.

"Any time you need to stop, just let me know."

She wrapped her arms around his middle. "Stop worrying about me. Really. I feel much better."

It was a good line, but Dec didn't believe it.

No question, something was really wrong because within minutes, she was leaning against him. Her body seemed almost boneless. And she felt warm. Too warm.

His heartbeat stuttered.

She couldn't be ill. Not now. Not when he had yet to get her home.

HE TOOK three-minute breaks every half hour, seating Annie in whatever shade he could find on this increasingly arid stretch of land, each time urging her to drink some water.

The fifth time she took a mouthful, she gagged and vomited it up.

"Sorry," she whispered. "So sorry."

"Hush." Dec shook his head and gently wiped her

mouth with the bandana. "It's the weather," he said, trying to convince himself as much as her. "Going from cold to warm, and now the wind picking up..."

"I'm okay."

"Are you sure? We can take another couple of minutes."

"I'm fine. And I know we have to keep moving."

She was right, of course, and they both knew it.

At noon, he spotted something on the horizon. Figures moving towards them. They had not seen another person since the dozing old guy they'd passed on their way to the sheepherder's shack.

Dec eased his Glock from its holster. There was no place to hide. Besides, he knew they'd already been spotted.

The figures drew closer. Two men and a boy, one man riding a mule, the other and the boy walking alongside.

Dec greeted them with a smile. They responded. It was all brief and polite, but it made him uneasy. If they were surprised to see a man and woman in camos riding a single horse, they didn't show it. Well, the boy did. Just a little. His eyes widened; he looked up at the man striding along next to him, but the man didn't acknowledge the child.

When they'd put a few yards between them, Dec glanced back. The men and the boy were staring after him and Annie.

Dec's gut tightened. The smart thing was to eliminate them, but to kill a child...

"What?" Annie said.

Dec forced a smile, raised his hand in salute. The strangers did the same, turned and kept going.

"Nothing," Dec said. "Can you go a little longer until we take another break?"

Annie said that she could and he pushed on for almost an hour before stopping.

She looked terribly sick. Her eyes were glassy. Her skin was dry and hot.

He sat her under the branches of a puny tree. It offered at least some shade, though not much. Then he tore a T-shirt almost in half, poured water over what was now a long strip of black cotton, and tied it around her forehead. She touched her fingers to the cloth and gave him a wobbly smile.

"The newes' fashion."

Her words were slurred. He was sure she was running a high fever. He dug into his gear, came up with a small packet of antibiotic capsules, tore the packet open and brought a capsule to her lips.

"Whass that?"

"An antibiotic. It'll make you feel better."

Dutifully, she opened her mouth and let him put the capsule on her tongue. Dec held the water bag to her lips.

"Just a tiny sip, honey."

That was all she took. A tiny sip. But she couldn't keep it down. Not the water. Not the antibiotic.

"Sorry," she gasped.

"Shh, Anoushka. There's nothing to be sorry for." Gently, Dec cleaned her face. Then he wrapped his arms around her and drew her onto his lap. "You have some kind of bug, that's all."

"Rotten timing," she whispered.

He couldn't argue with that.

And what could he do to help her?

He'd taken intensive first aid courses. He knew how to stop heavy bleeding, how to splint broken bones, even how to stitch a wound, but what did you do when the woman you loved was getting sicker by the minute and you were in the fucking middle of nowhere?

She needed fluids and meds. He had water, ibuprofen and an antibiotic, but they were all useless if she couldn't keep them down.

And they were running out of time.

They had to get to the extraction point. At most, there'd be a five to ten minute window for pickup. If Altair Amjad found them before then, there might not even be that much.

"Annie," Dec said softly. "Honey, we have to keep going."

She nodded. He got to his feet and drew her up with him. As soon as they were mounted, she put her arms around him and all but collapsed against his back.

Shit. Could she fall off?

Absolutely, she could.

He drew back on the reins, lifted his leg over the horse's head—not the safest way to dismount, but he was afraid to let Annie dismount by herself—and lifted her down. Then he remounted the horse, this time with Annie in his arms.

Riding double wasn't great in the best of circumstances. Riding double with her in front of him was even less efficient, but this way he could cradle her in his arms and keep her from falling.

Her head fell back against his chest.

He pressed his lips to her hair, told her that he loved her, and tapped his heels against the horse's flanks. His instinct was to urge the animal into a gallop, but he suspected the rough up-and-down motion might be bad for Annie.

He didn't want to risk her vomiting again.

It would only dehydrate her further.

He felt her weight against him increase, felt her breathing slow. Good. She was asleep. Rest might help her get through whatever illness had claimed her.

Hours went by.

The mountain they were going to cross loomed on the horizon, never seeming any closer. It didn't look terribly high. If it wasn't, if he could see an immediate, easy way up, they might still get out of this without running the risk of confrontation.

Normally, Dec would have welcomed the chance to face the enemy, but his first, his only priority was getting Annie over the mountain, to the coast—and home.

At last, the view began to change.

They were still riding through sparse vegetation, but now the landscape was also home to big boulders. A giant's chessboard, Dec thought as he looked around him. The view ahead was changing as well; he could he could see the mountain with greater clarity.

Shit.

It wasn't a promising sight.

They'd climbed a forested mountain a couple of days ago. It had made for doable if slow going.

What lay ahead was what could only be described as a slab of granite. A monolith, if you wanted to get fancy. A giant tombstone, if you didn't. No trees grew on it unless you counted a handful of skinny things that looked as if somebody had decided to create tortured bonsai.

No plants.

No grasses.

Just one motherfucking piece of stone.

Dec slowed the horse, tilted back his head and looked up.

"Fuck," he whispered.

Fuck, indeed.

He could see only one way up and it was little more than a series of possible handholds and footholds.

He clucked to the horse and they rode slowly along the base of the mountain for a little while—a little while was all they had to spare—before returning to where he'd started. What he'd seen at first, that series of miniscule fissures, was it.

Difficult, but yeah, he could manage. He'd had lots of climbing training and experience.

But that didn't matter.

Annie couldn't get up this thing. Yes, she was tough and she learned fast. He could use paracord to string them together, give her a five minute lesson in how to place her hands and feet, and maybe, *maybe* she could do it, but in the condition she was in?

Never.

The horse pawed at the ground. Dec patted the animal's neck to calm it.

The horse was uneasy. Did he sense something? Hear something? Animals sometimes picked up signs and signals humans didn't.

So what now? How the fuck were they going to cross this mountain?

Some kind of paracord sling to hoist Annie up? Forget it. He had no way to anchor a sling. Besides, slings had a nasty tendency to spin and bump and bang.

Running the risk of letting Annie slam into this wall of stone was out of the question.

A fireman's carry? A military lift? Also no good. No matter how careful he was, if he slung Annie over his shoulder, his center of gravity would be all wrong. He'd be fighting to keep the two of them from tumbling backwards into space and it would be a fight he—and she—would lose.

Dec took a deep breath, then exhaled slowly. He had to calm down, get centered. Think.

Think.

"Annie?"

She stirred in his arms. "Declan," she whispered.

Carefully, holding her close, he slid to the ground and trotted to the nearest boulder. He sat her down, her back against the boulder, went back to the horse and took his pack from where he'd hung it on the saddle.

"Sweetheart? How do you feel?"

She made a face. "Won'erful."

He forced a smile as he got out the water bag.

"Glad to hear it. Sit up a little. That's it. I want you to try and drink some water. "

"I'll prob'ly throw up."

"Just water, Annie. No pills. Nothing but water." He opened the. bag and brought it to her mouth. "Try a sip. Slowly. No rush."

She drank. A few drops only. He held his breath, damn near willing the water to stay down...

It didn't. It spewed straight out of her mouth.

She made a little sound of distress. "I'm sorry..."

"That's okay, baby. Don't worry about it." He took a dirty shirt from his pack, soaked it with water and gently applied it to her hot face.

"Mmm. Feels good."

"Yeah. I'm glad. Annie? Look at me."

She lifted her head and he patted her lips with the wet shirt. Her tongue came out; she licked at the drops. Yes! Why hadn't he thought of this sooner?

He was a big proponent of keeping hydrated. The need for fluids had been drummed into him in the SEALs as well as in STUD; time in the field had only reinforced the conviction that one of the worst enemies you could face was dehydration.

"A little more," he said softly, dabbing her lips with the wet shirt again.

"Nice," she whispered.

His belly clenched.

She looked like hell. The glassy eyes. The flushed skin. Even the way she was breathing. She was sick. Very sick.

The names of diseases common to this part of the world flashed through his head. Typhoid. Paratyphoid. MERS, short for Middle Eastern Respiratory Syndrome. Who knew what she might have picked up? Her kidnappers had kept her cuffed in that fucking filthy shed...

He had to get her home, fast. And, goddammit, he...

His satphone buzzed. Dec scrambled through his gear, pulled out the phone, pushed a button, barked his name.

"Sanchez here."

"Sanchez, this is Rescue Base."

Dec frowned. He didn't recognize the voice .

"I'm Colonel John Stuart. Do you recognize the name, Sanchez?"

Hell, yes, he recognized the name. Stuart had a reputation that went back to Operation Desert Storm. Now he served as liaison between Washington and a top secret committee with a bunch of letters for a name. Depending on who you listened to, he was either a tough, hard-nosed commander or a politically astute ass-kisser.

"Yessir, Colonel. I recognize it."

"Satellite surveillance tells us you're one climb and one descent from your objective. Correct?"

Dec nodded. The mountain, and then the coastal plain.

"Yessir. Correct."

"We need you to speed things up, son. Intel reports that your primary opponent is maybe thirty minutes from your location."

Dec nodded again. Amjad. The two men and the boy they'd passed hours before must have fingered them.

He looked at Annie. She was leaning back against the boulder. Her eyes were closed.

He rose and moved a few feet away. A gust of wind slapped at him; he looked up at the sky. Great. Amjad and the weather were both coming straight at them.

"Sanchez. Do you copy?"

"Copy, sir. But I have a problem."

"You sure as shit do, son. Didn't you understand me? They're closing in on you."

"No horses this time, I bet."

"Horses? Ah. I understand. No. No horses. Those bozos were locals, wanting to get in on the fun. You're facing maybe thirty men, several vehicles—American trucks, courtesy of some goddamn misguided committee's dumb-ass foreign aid package five or six years ago."

"Yessir."

"Well, get your shit together and move. Your opponent won't follow once you're on the other side of that mountain. You'll be in a sovereign state that's friendly to us when Washington tells them to be friendly. Your opponent doesn't have that kind of arrangement. He can't afford to screw with them."

Dec took a deep breath. "Sir. With all due respect, I can't do what you're asking."

Stuart's voice turned to ice. "What do you mean, you can't?"

"This thing ahead of us is one huge motherfucking chunk of rock. Begging your pardon, Colonel, but that's what it is. What isn't smooth as a baby's ass is basically nothing but a badly designed climbing wall."

"So? You have hands and feet, Sanchez. Use them."

"Not possible. Annie—the princess is sick, sir."

"How sick? Is she injured?"

"Not injured, no. She's running a high fever and she can't keep anything down."

"Crap!"

"Yessir."

"She can't get up that rock? Even with you helping her?"

"She can't stay on her feet, Colonel." Dec turned away and lowered his voice. "She's sick. Very sick. She's dehydrating. If I don't get her out of here soon..."

"Crap," Stuart said again. "She dies, we've got a fucking international incident on top of a fucking international incident."

Dec clenched his fist. An international incident? Was that what the possible death of the woman he loved meant to this idiot?

"We need to move fast, sir," Dec said, forcing the *sir* through his teeth. "Send in a couple of birds. One to take Annie—the princess—to safety, the other to lay down covering fire in case Amjad gets here while she'd still being extracted."

"Thank you for the advice, Lieutenant."

The rebuke was clipped and cold. Dec bit his lip. It was stupid to antagonize this jerk, and he knew it. So he waited, saying nothing until Stuart spoke again.

"Okay. Two birds in the air. With luck, ETA about five minutes before Amjad reaches you."

"Sir. One last thing." Dec cleared his throat. "She must not be returned to Qaram. Or taken to Tharsalonia. Once she's stable, fly her to the States. Her situation is..."

"Her situation," Stuart said, even more coldly, "is none of your concern."

"For Christ's sake, Colonel! Do the right thing!"

"You will report to me on your return to base, Sanchez."

Dec didn't answer. Whatever he said next might land him a court martial. What good would he be to Annie then?

"Did you hear me, Lieutenant? You will report to me on your return."

Dec took a breath. "Yessir."

"Not that you're entitled to an explanation, Lieutenant, but I have spent my entire life doing the right thing. I sure as shit don't have to be lectured on it by you!"

The line went dead.

Fuck. *Fuck!* Dec slammed down the satphone.

Do the right thing. The unofficial motto of the Units. Do it for God, for your country, for the guy fighting beside you. Do it because you believe in honor and duty and commitment.

Who knew what doing the right thing meant to a mired-in-DC-manure colonel?

Yeah, well, to hell with the colonel.

Dec would be on the Black Hawk with Annie. He'd be with her when it landed on the deck of the *Harry S. Truman*, the super-carrier stationed in the Gulf. He'd be with her when the docs on board checked her over, treated her, did whatever had to be done, he'd be with her during her return to the States, and he wouldn't need the permission of any candy-ass colonel to make sure everybody involved did the right thing.

Dec's mission had been to find Annie and get her to safety, and that mission wouldn't end until he brought her to American soil.

And Amjad the Deliverer was determined to keep that from happening.

Stuart had said the helicopters would arrive only a few minutes before the terrorists. Dec had to assume they wouldn't. Assuming the worst was always the safest bet.

A gust of wind sent a rush of dust and coarse sand slapping at his face. Visibility was getting poor. That would make it tough for the helicopters, but it might help him. And, dammit, he was running out of time.

A plan. He needed a fucking plan...

The first thing was to check his weapons. The HK MP7. The Glock. The SOG TAK knife. Ammo. Yeah, he still had plenty. The HK MP7 could fire 40 rounds without reloading.

Perfect.

The second thing was to move Annie. But where? There, to that cluster of boulders. Each was the size of a big car. The boulders would hide her as well as provide some protection.

He would take up a position behind a huge chunk of rock ten, twelve meters away where he could see her, keep her covered, but where he wouldn't be close enough for any enemy fire he took to endanger her.

The horse whinnied.

Hell. The animal would be an easy target. Dec undid the saddle, the bridle, tossed everything aside. What had Annie called him?

"Thanks for your help, Big Boy," Dec said softly.

Then he slapped the animal on the rump. "Hooy-ah," he yelled, and the horse took off.

He stiffened.

What was that? The wind made it difficult to hear, but...Engines. That was what he heard. Vehicles were coming in their direction.

So much for having thirty minutes.

Dec ran to where he'd left Annie and scooped her into his arms.

"Decl'n?"

"Yes, honey."

She buried her face against his throat. Her face, her body were hot. His heart thundered. Even her breath felt hot.

Quickly, he carried her to the boulders and sat her behind them.

"Annie. You're going to stay right here. No matter

what you hear, what you see, you're not to leave this place. Understand?"

"Yes." Tears glittered in her eyes. "I'm sorry. So sorry."

He crouched down and clasped her hands. "For what? There's nothing to be sorry for."

"So much trouble..."

"Trouble? You? You're never been trouble, Anoushka. Never."

"Are they coming?"

He wanted to lie. *No,* he'd say, *they're not. We're just going to wait here for our ride home...*

Instead, he let go of her hands and cupped her face . "Yes," he said bluntly. "But they're not going to get you."

"Who is it? Which of them is coming for us?"

Dec hesitated. "Amjad."

A tremor went through her. "He'll kill you," she whispered.

"Kill me?" He forced a laugh. "Hell, sweetheart, tougher bastards than a guy with a lice-infested beard have tried to kill me. And I'm still here."

"I love you, Declan. I love you, love you, love—"

He kissed her with a hunger that was soul-deep. How could he have ever thought she'd willingly left him? He should have searched for her even it meant going to the ends of the universe.

"We're going to get through this, honey. We have a lifetime to spend together. I won't let anybody take that from us."

"I know you'll do everything you can to save us."

She drew an unsteady breath. "But if—if things should go wrong...."

She was right. Things could go wrong. It would be stupid not to acknowledge that.

Dec took his Glock from its holster and put on the ground next to her.

"Remember the trigger safety," he said, looking straight into her eyes. "Pull, then fire."

Annie was crying. "I know," she whispered.

"Don't use the gun except to defend yourself." He paused, knowing his next words would be the most difficult he'd ever spoken. "And only, *only* if you know there's no choice left, if I'm down and you're absolutely certain that everything is lost..."

His heart rose into his throat. There was no mistaking the throaty growl of Amjad's oncoming vehicles.

"Annie. It's time. Get down. Stay down. And never forget that I love you."

Annie flung herself into his arms for one last kiss. It tasted of dreams and despair, of hope and sorrow, of a love that would last through eternity.

Then Dec scrambled to his feet, ran to the rock that was going to be his line of defense and threw himself down behind it.

The wind was blowing hard. The air was thick with dust, but Amjad's raiding party was now close enough so Dec could count the oncoming vehicles. Two trucks. Three. Jesus. Six altogether, strung out in a line and racing towards him and Annie and the mountain.

Nothing subtle in their approach either. The terrorists couldn't have spotted him yet, but they knew he was there and they were making the most of showing him that he was outnumbered and outgunned.

Dec checked his rifle. He was a good shot. Forget that. He was one hell of a shot. He'd hold his fire until the last second, then take out those fucking headlights. Then the windshields. With luck, he'd blow up the drivers...

Whomp-whomp-whomp.

He looked up. Two Black Hawks, coming in fast.

Dec grinned. The cavalry to the rescue. He could feel his adrenaline pumping.

Everything was happening at once. It was either going to be a massive fuckup or a massive win—and only someone who'd never been a SEAL or a STUD would dare think it would be anything but a win.

The vehicles were getting closer. Closer. Suddenly, one veered to the right. Towards where he had hidden Annie.

An old childhood phrase danced in his head.

Ready or not, here I come.

Dec rose up on his knees, rested his HK MP7 on top of the rock, and fired.

13

The Black Hawks emerged like alien war machines from the dust-filled sky.

"Fuck," Chay Olivieri shouted. "Amjad beat us to it."

"Hold your fire," Nick Romano yelled. "Sanchez and Annie are down there somewhere. We got to identify them before—"

Aidan Maguire pounded on Nick's shoulder. "Got 'em," he said. "Dec's at one o'clock. Annie's at ten."

"Where?" Danny Sullivan said. "I don't—"

"She's in among those big rocks," Alex Spanos said. "See her?"

Chay peered out the open door. Then he pumped his fist in the air.

"Rescue Two," he said into his mike. "We have eyes on them both. Our man at one o'clock. The lady at ten. Please confirm."

"Rescue One. Confirmed. Warrior at one, lady at ten. Going in for the lady."

Danny laughed. "Sounds like a fucking scene from King Arthur."

"Who?" said Nick, but he grinned when he said it.

Chay tapped the pilot on the shoulder. "Take us down," he said, mirroring the words with a lowering of his hand.

The pilot nodded and Rescue One began dropping. . Lower. Lower. Lower...

Lines fell from the helicopter and the five STUD operatives rappelled to the ground while the remaining men on board opened covering fire. Dec saw them coming, grinned and provided covering fire.

Two trucks went up in flames. Insurgents in one of the trucks flung open the doors.

Dec took them out.

Yes, the timing still sucked, but the playing field was evening up. STUD One was here. Even in full combat gear, Dec recognized his brothers as they sprinted towards him, firing as they ran, taking out the enemy and drawing attention from the rescue bird to themselves.

Whoosh!

Another truck went up in a ball of flame. A couple of men stumbled out of the back, shooting as they ran. Dec fired and took them both down. Only two trucks remained in the clearing now, but Dec, the gunship and the STUD operatives were taking them out with cold efficiency.

Dec flashed at look to where he'd left Annie.

A soldier hanging onto a hoist was dropping from the rescue bird.

Dec got to his feet and sprinted towards it. Something hot sizzled past his ear. He swung around fast, saw the fucker who'd fired at him...

Bang!

Somebody put the guy down, and fast. Dec spun around...

Not somebody.

Annie. She was on her feet, arms extended, still holding the Glock in a two-handed grip.

"Annie!"

Dec reached her, pried the Glock from her fingers and pulled her down to her knees with him.

"Annie, goddammit, you could have been killed!"

"He was going to shoot you, Declan. He was going to kill you."

Her teeth were chattering. Her entire body was shaking. Dec cursed and gathered her against him, held her to his pounding heart.

The guy from the Black Hawk was right next to him. "Dude," he said, grabbing Dec's shoulder, "I gotta get the lady out of here."

"No," Annie said, "not without you!"

Dec knew the promise he'd made, but they were in the middle of a fire fight. Her safety was all that mattered.

She had to go out first.

"Anoushka. Get in the hoist."

"Not without you! You said—"

Shots whizzed by. Declan and the soldier who'd descended from the Black Hawk both spun and fired; Nick and Chay raced up and joined in.

"Get her out of here," Dec yelled to the soldier from the rescue bird.

"No," Annie said. "Declan, don't—"

He shoved her into the hoist and secured it. The rescue guy grabbed onto the line, looked up and signaled.

The line began to rise. It went up, up, up...

Hands reached out and pulled Annie to safety. Her rescuer vanished inside the Black Hawk with her.

The helicopter pulled away and quickly gained altitude.

Dec stared after it. The sounds of the battle faded.

All he could think of was Annie.

They were separated again. But this time, it wouldn't be for long. It would take time for the docs to evaluate her once she was on the super-carrier, time to stabilize her before flying her home.

He'd be with her long before that—

Chay knocked him to the ground. "Dude," he yelled, "you want to play at being a target or you want to finish these fuckers off?"

"Amjad?" Dec asked.

Chay shook his head. "Not among the party-goers."

Another burst of small-arms fire made both men roll to their sides.

"Go," Dec shouted, and crouching and weaving, he, Chay and Nick ran back to deal with the remaining insurgents.

～

AN HOUR LATER, Rescue Two settled on the deck of the *Harry S. Truman.*

The end of the fight had been predictable. Amjad's fighters hadn't been able to stand up to the fire power unleashed by the guys on the Black Hawk and those on the ground. The ones that hadn't gone down had fled. That their leader had not been with them was a disappointment, but taking out this bunch had been a real victory. They were the terrorist leader's elite strike force and this had been an embarrassing defeat for him.

Only one of the Americans had been wounded. A bullet had plowed a shallow flesh wound in Aidan Maguire's thigh.

"Good thing it didn't hit further up," Danny Sullivan said solemnly. "I mean, dude, what did that shot take out? Two inches of skin? Hell, you'd be dickless."

Everybody laughed, including Dec, though his laughter was tempered by a growing sense of anxiety.

All he could think about was Annie.

The men clambered out of the bird and headed for one of the flight deck elevators. Dec knew he was expected to join them. So far, nobody had asked what had happened to him during the last few days, but he knew they were curious. They had questions and they were entitled to answers. Plus, aside from a standard mission debriefing, Colonel Stuart had ordered Dec to report to him immediately.

But all that would have to wait until he saw Annie.

He needed to be sure she was okay, that the docs had begun whatever treatment she required...

Dammit. He needed to hold her in his arms.

The elevator doors closed. Dec reached out and hit the button for deck two.

Alex Spanos shook his head. "That's the medical deck. Debriefing's on—"

"I know. I'll be there in five."

"Listen, dude, the guy running this show, this Colonel Stuart, is a real hard-ass."

"Got that." The elevator stopped and the doors slid open. "Five minutes, that's all." He looked at the faces of the men he loved like brothers and saw worry in their eyes. "I promised the princess...I promised Annie..." Dec cleared his throat. "I have to see her, okay? That's it."

He stepped out. The doors shut and the remaining five STUDs looked at each other.

"He's got it bad," Maguire said.

Romano blew out a breath. "Real bad."

"Remind me never to let a woman get her hooks in me," Sullivan added.

All the guys nodded. All except Chay.

He knew this wasn't about getting hooked. It was about finding the half of yourself you hadn't even known was missing, and that was impossible to explain to any man who hadn't been there, done that.

A few months back, he'd shocked himself, shocked pretty much everybody who knew him, by falling in love and getting married, which was probably why only he understood that Sanchez was willing to risk an official reprimand to make sure his woman was okay.

Only problem was that Dec's woman was a princess.

You had to think that might tend to complicate things.

~

"What do you mean, she isn't here?"

Dec was standing toe to toe with a corpsman. The kid, nineteen on a good day and with a bunch of peach fuzz trying to set up shop on his rotund baby face, was visibly intimidated.

No surprise there.

Dec had at least four inches in height on the boy, at least twenty pounds of muscle, and enough attitude to catapult an F-18 off the flight deck without any additional help. Plus he knew that he probably smelled pretty bad—he'd been wearing the same clothes for who knew how long and now blood had been added to the stink of dirt and sweat.

So, yeah. The kid was intimidated. And that was fine with Dec. He'd been passed from corpsman to corpsman, each one telling him no, there was no Princess Anoushka here; no Annie Stanton; no civilian, female or otherwise, who'd been brought in by helicopter during the past couple of hours, during the past week, the past month...

Bullshit.

Maybe this had to do with security. Yes. That made sense. Annie was a princess. She was, as Stuart had put it, at the center of an international incident.

Dec took half a step back. He'd give the kind a little breathing room.

"Okay, son, I get that this is a security issue. Get me the officer on duty. He'll clear this up."

"Sir. This isn't a security issue. It isn't one because there's no Anna Stanley—"

"Annie Stanton," Dec said in a dangerously flat voice.

"That's what I meant, sir. She isn't here. No princesses, either. I don't know who told you somebody like that would be here, sir, but—"

"I'll handle this, corpsman."

The kid shot up straight. Dec could almost hear his heels click together.

"Sir. Yessir."

Dec turned to get a look at the man who'd caused such a reaction. The guy was tall and thin, with an equally thin mouth. Hell. It was Stuart. Who else would be wearing an army uniform adorned with silver eagles on board a US Navy ship?

"Corpsman," Stuart barked. "Dismissed."

The kid started to salute, apparently realized you weren't supposed to salute indoors, managed a hoarse *Yessir* and scurried away. Stuart had not taken his eyes off Dec. His gaze was cold, focused, and accusatory.

"What are you doing here, Lieutenant?"

"Sir. I came to check on the princess."

"Did I not order you to report to me as soon as you boarded this ship?"

"You did, sir. But I promised the princess..."

Stuart did a classic about-face. "Follow me," he snapped.

"Colonel Stuart. I was assigned a mission. It involved the welfare of—"

The colonel swung back towards Dec. "How does ten days in the brig sound?"

"The welfare of the princess is my responsibility!"

"Twenty days," Stuart snapped. "And if you think I won't do it, just try me."

The man meant what he said. That was clear. Dec was almost uncontrollably angry, but what good would he be to Annie if he was locked up?

Stuart strode away. Dec had no choice. He followed.

Three minutes and several decks later, they were inside a small office. A desk, two chairs, a file cabinet. Nothing distinguished it from any other office Dec had ever been in except the slim gold laptop computer that sat on the desk.

Stuart sat down. Opened the computer and glowered at the screen. Dec stood across from him, his posture stiff. He knew that keeping him standing this way, unacknowledged and silent, was deliberate.

Did the colonel consider himself an expert at tactical games? If he did, he'd never had a STUD for an opponent.

Seconds passed.

Dec kept his cool. He concentrated on thinking about Annie, what he'd tell her when they finally let him see her, how it would be when they were in California, when they began their new life together...

"It may interest you to know that the princess will be fine."

Dec let out a breath. Stuart had yet to make eye contact.

"She has a virus. Nothing untreatable. In fact, I have word that she'll be up and about in a day or two."

Dec nodded. "Thank you."

"Thank you, *sir* ."

"Thank you, sir."

Silence. Stuart kept looking at his computer screen. Finally, he closed the computer and raised his eyes to Dec.

"Did you actually believe you had a future with the Princess of Qaram?"

"Is the colonel asking for a discussion of my personal beliefs?"

"You had an order. You were to free the Americans and bring them to safety."

"We accomplished our mission. One American was dead by the time we reached the target. We rescued the remaining three."

"Did you hear what I said, Sanchez? You were to bring them to safety."

"Which we did."

"Which we did, *sir*."

Dec had been staring at the wall above the

colonel's head. Now, he brought his gaze straight to the man's face

"Which we did, *sir*."

"Incorrect. Five men in your unit delivered the ambassador and his wife to safety. You led the princess further into danger."

"I did not."

"Did you put her on board the helicopter with the ambassador and his wife?"

Dec didn't answer.

"Did you instead take her into the mountains where she was attacked by ta pair of killers?"

"She was not attacked, Colonel. I dealt with—"

"Did she spend two nights and three days in a godforsaken wilderness with you where anything could have happened to her?"

"Colonel. You don't know the whole—"

Stuart shot to his feet.

"Did you take her into a situation in which she faced capture by the terrorist Altair Amjad?"

"Goddammit, Colonel, it wasn't like that! She begged me not to put her on the helicopter with the ambassador. She begged me not to send her back to her uncle. She—"

"She begged you," Stuart sneered.

Dec could feel his face heat. "Yes. She begged me. Do you have any idea what her uncle had done to her? What he'd planned to do with her? If you'd just listen—"

"Your mission is over, Sanchez. You and the rest of your unit are flying out at tonight at twenty-one-thirty."

The colonel's eyes narrowed. "If you were part of my command, I would have you court-martialed, but your commanding officer has requested disciplining you be left to him. Out of respect for him, I have agreed." Stuart took his seat and opened his computer. "Dismissed."

"Where is Anoushka?"

"I said, dismissed!"

Dec leaned forward and slammed his hands on the desk. "Where is she?"

Stuart's face turned purple. "Who the hell do you think you are?"

"I'm a man who made a promise. A STUD operative who made a promise. Where is Annie Stanton?"

The colonel picked up his telephone. "I want Security here immediately!"

"Where is she, Stuart? If you sent her back to her uncle, Jesus Christ, if you sent her to him—"

The door flew open. Hands grabbed Dec's elbows. Lifted him off his feet. Carried him backwards out the door and into the narrow hall.

"Let go of me," Dec snarled. "Goddammit..."

"Shut up, Sanchez," a familiar voice growled. "Just shut the fuck up."

Dec blinked. "Olivieri?"

"Olivieri," Chay said. "And Spanos. The others are right behind us. You keep fighting, we'll keep your arms, they'll take your feet and we'll carry you out of her like a package. Is that what you want?"

Dec's shoulders slumped. "Shit!"

"Yeah. Exactly. Maguire? Get that door."

Chay and Alex, with Dec locked between them and the others hard on their heels, stepped into a room. It was some kind of break room—a coffee pot, a platter of doughnuts, a couple of tables and some chairs—and a surprised-looking sailor with a doughnut in her hand.

Aidan Maguire glared at her. "Out," he barked.

The sailor scurried out the door. Danny Sullivan kicked it shut while Chay and Alex dropped Dec in a chair. A second later, Sullivan, Olivieri, Spanos, Maguire and Romano stood around Dec in a semicircle, all of them glowering, all with their feet apart and their arms folded over their chests.

"Sanchez," Spanos demanded, "what the fuck did you think you were doing?"

Dec rubbed his hands over his face. "Okay. I was a little out of line."

Sullivan raised his eyebrows. "A little?"

"Stuart is an asshole!"

The men looked at each other. "What a revelation," Olivieri said.

'Yeah," Maguire said, "we can always count on Sanchez to figure out the tough stuff."

"He's also a colonel connected to the DOD, to State, to CIA and NSA...dammit, he's probably got a hotline straight into the Oval Office." Romano shook his head. "He didn't just want to throw you to the wolves, Dec, he wanted to stand by and watch them rip you apart."

Dec rested his arms on his thighs and looked down at the floor.

"Yeah. I guess."

"You guess? You *guess*?"

"Okay. You're right." Dec looked up. "You guys saved my ass."

Olivieri shook his head. "Black saved your ass."

"Black?"

"Stuart contacted him. Told him you were—what's the quote, Danny?"

"An undisciplined, dangerous, out-of-control misfit."

"But that you were handsome," Aidan said.

The lame joke broke the tension. Everybody laughed, even Dec. Then his laughter faded.

"Fuck," he said softly.

"Fuck's the word, dude." Spanos rolled his eyes. "Black said yup, you were all that and more."

"Great."

"But he also said you had a chest full of fruit salad and he knew Stuart wouldn't want the press to somehow learn that an army officer who'd washed out of Delta Force twenty years ago had brought charges against a highly decorated Special Ops hero."

Dec sat up straight. "What?"

Romano shrugged his shoulders. "Seems our captain and the colonel knew each other way back when."

Dec grinned. "Go figure."

"Exactly. Go figure."

More silence. Then Dec looked from one of his buddies to the other. Each of them made eye contact, then looked away. He figured the question he was going to ask might as well have been tattooed on his forehead.

"Where is she?" he said softly.

Throats were cleared. Feet were shuffled. Looks were exchanged.

"Chay? Where's Annie?"

Chay Olivieri sighed. "They never brought her here, Dec. They flew her straight to Qaram."

14

U nit One was on American soil less than eighteen hours later.

The five members of Unit One who'd gotten out together had reported to their captain by Skype three days ago.

Now he wanted another report? On the firefight? Maybe, but they all doubted it.

This would be about what had gone wrong on their primary mission.

Everybody knew it.

Black texted them while they were heading home. He said they'd have twenty minutes to shower, change clothes, grab coffee—whatever they could do in that time frame—and then report to his office.

The captain was waiting for them in the big, handsome office that been the library in what had once been a palatial private residence on the beach at Santa Barbara. The view out the windows was incredible: the long stretch of beach, the waves lapping against the shore. A ceiling fan rotated slowly over-head; coffee and sandwiches were laid out on a side table

Their CO's desk held center stage.

Normally, you'd stand before that desk when you were summoned here. Or Black would wave a hand at one of a pair of chairs drawn up before it.

Not this time.

Half a dozen metal folding chairs stood lined up before the desk. They were lined up with precision, and, Dec knew, with intent.

This would not be a comfortable meeting.

Black was seated behind his desk. Everything about him whispered *command*, from his neatly-cropped greying hair to his crisp uniform. His hands were folded on the top of a stack of papers.

His expression was grim.

"Maguire, shut the door. All of you, sit down."

So much for cordial greetings.

They sat.

Black said nothing.

The seconds ticked away.

Dec had some training in interrogation techniques. They all did, which mean they all knew what their CO was doing: he was reinforcing the facts. He was in charge. They were essentially powerless. Whatever took place next was under his control.

Still, knowing all that didn't much help.

Dec was uncomfortable; he knew the other guys were equally uncomfortable. It was that old routine of waiting for the other shoe to drop.

The one difference was, he and Chay, Nick, Aidan, Alex and Danny were well-trained.

They knew how vital it was to wait for that shoe to drop. Black knew it too, which meant it was a relief—a very small one, but still a relief—when he finally made a move.

He pushed back his chair and rose from his desk.

The men from Unit One started to shoot to their feet. Black held up a hand and motioned them back.

"I'm told your flight home was uneventful."

Nobody responded.

"I've read the debriefing reports on the firefight."

Still no response.

"Twenty-eight insurgents killed. Four wounded. Nicely done."

Silence.

"And the princess extracted. Again, nicely done."

No one so much as blinked.

"I do have some questions. Not a lot, just some—but we can get to those another time." Black strolled to the window and looked out. "Right now, I have another topic to discuss."

A faint, ever-so-faint shuffling of feet.

"It's about what went down four days ago. Your removal of the princess and two others from the camp where they were being held captive." Black turned to look at the men, arms folded across his chest. "To be more specific, I'm interested in what happened at the point of extraction. Maguire. Sullivan. Spanos. Olivieri. Romano."

"Sir!" Five voices barked as one.

"All of you managed to get on the Black Hawk that had been sent to extract you. All five of you, plus the ambassador and his wife. Is that correct?"

"Yessir."

Black turned his gaze on Dec.

Dec drew a long breath into his lungs. Here it was. The entire purpose of this meeting.

"And then we come to you, Sanchez. Somehow, you and Princess Anoushka just couldn't get to the bird all of your compatriots managed to reach. Am I correct again?

Dec exhaled. Raised his chin. Looked directly at his commanding officer.

"We could have reached it, sir. I chose not to do so."

Black's eyes narrowed. "So when your friends told me you hadn't been able to get to the Black Hawk in time, they were lying?"

"It's what they believed to be true, sir. They had no way of knowing I had decided that the princess and I would not go with them."

Not a lie. Just a twisting of the truth. Would Black accept it? Dec waited. Finally, Black strode to his desk and sat down behind it.

"Sanchez. Stay where you are. The rest of you are dismissed."

Spanos, Maguire, Sullivan, Romano and Olivier got to their feet. All of them looked at Dec.

"Sir," Romano said, "maybe we could—"

"Out!"

"Yessir, captain, but we were talking on the flight home and Lieutenant Sanchez told us that—"

"OUT!"

The men left. Black waited until he and Dec were alone. Then he looked at Dec.

"Sanchez."

"Yessir."

Black slammed his fist on his desk. The stack of papers scattered.

"What the *fuck* were you thinking? You had a clear mission. You were sent to rescue four Americans. You got to where you were supposed to go, slipped into that camp, discovered on American was a casualty, found and freed the others, took out a handful of human slime, got the captives and yourselves through rough country and to our rescue helicopter when all the odds were against you, evaded a band of lunatics who tried to kill you—and then you grabbed a horse—a *horse*—and rode off into the sunset with the Royal Princess of Qaram." Black shot to his feet. "What the fuck, Sanchez? Did you think you were starring in an old movie? Were you John Wayne? Errol Flynn? Jesus, don't look so blank. How about something more recent. Daniel Day Lewis? That name ring a bell?"

"Sir. Captain Black. I know how it looks..."

"How it looks," Black said tightly, "is like grounds for court-martial."

Dec didn't say anything. What *could* he say? How could he argue with that?

"So I'm waiting, Sanchez. Tell me what happened. Why you did what you did. I know you'd had prior involvement with this woman. Did the prospect of being alone with her for a farewell fuck mean so much?"

Dec was out of his chair before Black had finished the sentence. "If you weren't wearing that uniform..."

"Answer the question, Lieutenant. Were your actions personally motivated—or did you do what you believed it necessary to do?"

"I have more respect for my unit, for the men I serve with, than to have done something like that." His eyes narrowed. "And I have more respect for Annie—for the Princess Anoushka—than to let anyone talk about her that way."

Black sighed. He sat down, folded his hands and looked at Dec.

"You disobeyed orders, Sanchez."

Dec started to say that he had not—but he had. He'd been charged with freeing the hostages. He had done that—and then he'd gone further, strictly on his own.

He felt sick to his stomach. He was finished in the Units. Finished in the service. If he was lucky, he'd be allowed to resign, but it was more than likely he would receive a dishonorable discharge.

And yet, if it meant saving Annie from a life of servitude, he'd have made the same choices all over again.

Black jerked his chin at the chair Dec had abandoned. "Sit down, son," he said quietly.

Dec, head reeling, fell back into the chair.

"You love this woman."

There was no sense in denying the truth. Dec nodded. "Yessir. I do."

"And she loves you."

"She does."

"And you want to be together."

Dec nodded a third time.

"But that wasn't why you disobeyed orders and rode off with her, was it?"

"No. No sir. It wasn't." He looked at Black. "She was in terrible trouble. She still is. She was a pawn in an ugly game, an American citizen snatched from American soil—"

"Snatched? As in taken against her will?"

"Yessir." Black sighed. He picked up his phone and told his aide he wasn't to be interrupted. Then he nodded at Dec.

"Tell me everything, Sanchez. Start right at the beginning, and don't leave anything out."

So Dec told him.

He began with what Annie had divulged to him about the death of her parents and the takeover of the government by her uncle Cyrus. He spoke of the warning not to return home that had come from one of her father's most trusted advisor. He explained her quiet, anonymous existence Santa Barbara.

He spoke calmly until he got to the part about two men entering her apartment, kidnapping her and flying her back to Qaram.

When he reached that point, Dec could almost feel the rush of adrenaline in his body.

He got to his feet, paced as he talked, as he

related her imprisonment by her uncle, her uncle's plans to invade the oil-rich kingdom of Suwaith on Qaram's southern border, his bargain with the king of Tharsalonia that Tharsalonia would not oppose Qaram's invasion if Annie were given to him as his wife.

"So Annie Stanton was to be used to give Qaram's ruler carte blanche in an invasion of a sovereign nation, and the only reason that didn't happen was because bandits kidnapped her for sale to the terrorist Altair Amjad," Black shook his head. "I can see why she wasn't eager to be sent back to Qaram."

"Yessir," Dec said. "No way could I let that happen. There was no time to consult with you or—"

"You were in possession of information vital to our national interests, especially the planned invasion of Suwaith. You surely know we have interests and commitments there."

"Oil," Dec said bluntly.

"Oil," Black agreed. "And the fact that Suwaith is a fairly stable nation in an area known for its instability. Didn't you think any of that would be important to report?"

"Yes. Of course I did. But first I had to get Annie— the princess—out of harm's way."

"And you reached this conclusion, how?"

"My mission was to get her to safety. And as I saw it, that meant keeping her from being returned to Qaram."

"Because?"

"Because, sir, it was the right thing to do."

Silence filled the room. Then Black got to his feet again.

"In other words, your realized that returning the princess to her uncle would enable him to move forward with his plans to use her to form an alliance with Tharsalonia."

Dec nodded. True enough, but that hadn't really factored into his decision. He wasn't going to lie about it just to protect himself.

"I was aware of that, sir, but—"

"You concluded that as long as you kept the princess out of the game, so to speak, her uncle could not formalize that alliance."

"Yessir. But.—"

"And you recognized the importance of finding ways to prevent the invasion of Suwaith so that we would not be drawn into an armed engagement."

"All true, Captain, but my primary concern was—"

"Finally, you factored in Amjad's intention to acquire the princess for himself. You hoped that if you disrupted his plan, he might lose face, even show himself and be vulnerable to capture." Black's words were unhurried. Deliberate. Spoken in the same unemotional way he might have delivered them in a report. "All intelligent conclusions, Lieutenant. No one could fault you for acting on them, especially when you had to make your decisions in the heat of battle."

"Sir. I understand what you're doing, and I'm very grateful. But getting me off the hook changes nothing for Annie." A muscle knotted in Dec's jaw. "She's in grave danger, sir, perhaps even more danger than before now that she—now that she spent time alone with me. Her uncle may see her as—as damaged, by the tenets of Qaram's culture. She may have lost her value to him..."

Dec couldn't go on. If Annie's uncle assumed she'd had a lover, if he forced a physical exam on her, who knew where his rage might lead?

Black went to his desk, picked up a pen and rolled it between his fingers.

"You've unknowingly defined the current situation., Lieutenant."

"The current situation?"

"Your princess is up shit's creek," the captain said bluntly. "Intel's been coming in almost faster than we can process it. For starters, you are correct in your conclusion that the Tharsalonian king no longer wants Anoushka. Therefore, her uncle has decided she should be used in a different fashion."

Dec's heart thudded. "What does that mean?"

"The deal the bandits made with Amjad is now Cyrus's deal. Apparently, Amjad doesn't care if the princess spent time alone with you." His face tightened. "In fact, the son of a bitch seems to think her possible involvement with an American Special Ops warrior adds to her desirability. Some sort of convoluted slap in our face, as it were."

Dec dragged air into his lungs. "No. That can't happen."

"In return for the princess, Amjad will aid in the invasion of Suwaith. He and his men will then have a sovereign state as their base— and a steady supply of oil to fund their activities."

Dec's head was spinning. Amjad with an entire oil-rich nation in his back pocket was bad news, but all he could think about was Annie in the hands of the terrorist. His reputation for barbaric cruelty was unsurpassed.

"There is, however, one bright spot in all of this."

The captain's voice seemed far away. Whatever he was saying was unimportant. Annie was all that mattered. No way could he let her fall into Amjad's hands. He would go to her. Free her. No matter what it took. He could get into Qaram. Into the palace. He could get Annie the hell out. It wouldn't be easy, but he had an intricate skill set and he didn't have to wear a uniform to utilize those skills.

It would also mark him as a renegade. The life he loved in STUD would be over, but what did that matter when he could save Annie?

"Captain," Dec said abruptly, "there's no easy way to say this." He paused, aware that his next words would be irrevocable. "Being in this division...It means everything to me, sir. I'm proud to serve with you and the men in the Units. I'm proud of what we do. But I'm going to have to tender my—"

"Dammit, Lieutenant," Black said, tossing aside the pen, "have you heard a word I said? Cyrus's plans for his country have leaked to the Qarami underground. It's a group loyal to the former king, and it's been waiting in the wings for a long time. They're organized. Ready to establish a democratic interim government.

All they need is some help in removing Cyrus from the throne."

"That's good news, I'm sure, sir, but by the time that happens—"

"Amjad is coming for the princess in four days. That's just ninety-six hours. Cyrus is playing it quietly—he knows there's strong opposition to him and he didn't want the populace to be aware of his plan to link forces with Amjad, but the word got out anyway. The Qarami opposition is determined to stop him."

Dec's face had gone white. "Annie, handed over to the Deliverer? Never. Not while I'm still alive."

"Goddammit, Sanchez, stop being such a fucking idiot! What, you have some romantic picture of yourself as a renegade?"

"You don't understand. I can't let this happen."

"*You* can't let it happen? *We* can't let it happen! A terrorist lunatic invading Suwaith? Suwaith is our ally. We would have no choice but to put boots on the ground in its defense."

Dec stared at his CO, who took a deep breath.

"Intel advises that Amjad and a fifty man escort escort will appear at the palace in Qaram in four days. I need six men with cool heads to get into the palace, neutralize Cyrus and hand him over to the Qarami opposition for trial. I need those same six men to capture and bring back for interrogation a terrorist who is of great interest to our government." Black paused. "And if, in the process, those six men find and free an American citizen who is in being held captive and bring her home, they would have our government's thanks."

It took a few seconds before Dec understood what he'd been offered. He wanted to leap to his feet and cheer.

Instead, he nodded.

"Yessir," he said calmly. "That sounds like a plan to me."

"Yes," Black said dryly. "I thought it might." He flashed something that was almost a smile. "Get some sleep, put some food in your belly, and I'll see you and the rest of Unit One back here in precisely four hours."

15

They had less than three and a half days to put together a plan before they'd have to enact it.

Black gave the plan the code name *Renegade.* He said the name with a straight face, but not before his gaze lingered briefly on Declan.

Chay's reaction to the time crunch was succinct. "Fuck," he said.

That about summed it up.

But they weren't new to this. They'd worked under tighter deadlines, and cooperation from Black, from the alphabet-soup agency that had final approval over the mission as well as a tight liaison with the coalition of freedom fighters forming up inside Qaram helped grease the skids.

What they came up with was something basic. No bells or whistles—but it did have a lot of moving parts.

The so-called wedding of Princess Anoushka and the terrorist Altair Amjad would take place on Day Four at twenty-two hundred hours Qarami time.

At seventeen-hundred hours, a helicopter would fly STUD One out of an isolated airfield in a small, friendly country, its identity shielded by the name Renegade Base. The helicopter would be a Black Hawk equipped with the newest Stealth technology. It would drop them a mile from the palace in high desert country.

They would reach their final destination on foot.

A mile was nothing to men who did ten and fifteen mile training runs in full gear.

The important thing was to know as much as possible about their target location.

Satellite photos showed that the palace stood in splendid isolation on a hill with a commanding view of the ancient city below. The palace had been built five hundred years earlier, but Annie's father had made changes that moved it into the twenty-first century:.

Thanks to Dec, they knew much more.

He'd rolled up his metaphorical sleeves and gone back to something he'd always been good at.

He'd hacked into the sophisticated computer system that ran the palace.

He'd pulled up classified schematics, graphs and charts until they could virtually see inside the ancient walls.

They knew the location of the guard stations as well as entry and egress points. They knew the palace contained twenty-six bedrooms and thirty-four bathrooms, a library, a ballroom, a state dining room, a throne room, and a seemingly endless number of meeting rooms. The servants' quarters were on the fourth level; the enormous kitchen was in the basement.

They also had detailed information about the planned event that would link the interests of Amjad and Cyrus, most of it from the Qarami Freedom Fighters. Their leaders had been advisors to Annie's father. They were eager to see their false king stand trial on a public stage, and to implement the democracy Annie's father had intended.

From them, they learned that Annie's suite was on the second floor. So was her uncle's. A long corridor separated one set of rooms from the other.

Both suites were protected by members of Cyrus's private guard, men who were loyal to him. STUD One would deal with them; the Freedom Fighters would take care of the guards not on duty.

Amjad would have a suite on the same floor, guarded by his own men. STUD One would take them out—they were looking forward to it. The Freedom Fighters would deal with the others.

The best news was the discovery of an underground tunnel that led from what had once been a fort to a door in what looked like an unused part of the basement. hoped. The service stairs were maybe fifty feet away.

"Not gonna be too many people going up and down to the kitchen that hour of the night," Alex said.

"The tunnel's probably an old escape route," Dec said. He stabbed his finger at the map. "That's how we'll get in and get out."

"Assuming the tunnel entrance is accessible," Aidan said.

Dec picked up the phone and called Black. Black listened, then picked up his own phone. Two hours later they had an eyes-on response. The tunnel entrance, though all but buried behind overgrowth, was still there. Could it be accessed? Well, they'd just have to wait and find out.

Other data came from social media.

"Amazing," Romano said, "the stuff people put online."

Amjad had posted a snapshot of himself grinning and cradling an automatic rifle in his arms under the caption *Happy Surprises Coming.*

"What an asshole," Maguire said.

"He's right, though," Dec said with grim certainty. "He sure as hell has surprises coming."

Not all of what they needed was out there, but there was enough so that you could play connect-the-dots and come up with valid information.

And when you couldn't... Dec to the rescue again, with hacker talents that left the other guys grinning. It turned out that little was really private in today's world.

"Hack and ye shall find," Spanos said, and though they all laughed, they agreed it was true.

The plan was to get in fast, silence Cyrus and hand him over to the Freedom Fighters, grab Amjad, then free Annie. They'd go out the way they came in—through the tunnel—and once they were back on board the Black Hawk, the Freedom Fighters would get the signal that they could move ahead with their own plans for Cyrus and for Amjad's men.

STUD One worked around the clock, taking breaks only to workout in the training room or run on the beach. Those physical outlets kept them in shape, mentally as well as physically. They grabbed sleep in short doses and ate seated around a conference table in a room that adjoined Black's office, surrounded by computers, printers spewing endless sheets of paper, stacks of scribbled notes., and empty fast food containers.

On Day Three, they sat back, yawned, stretched, and agreed they had everything they could get.

Maguire nodded. "We've gone in with less."

Yes. They sure as hell had.

The final piece to nail down was how to make sure that Cyrus was still in his rooms when STUD One came through the tunnel.

After some back and forth between STUD One and the Freedom Fighters, it was agreed that Cyrus— Uncle Shit, as STUD One had dubbed him—would discover a button missing from his tuxedo jacket right before it was time to leave his suite and meet with Amjad.

It turned out that Uncle Shit wasn't only a villainous bastard, he was a stickler for sartorial perfection.

His valet would have to make a repair.

The valet, of course, was a member of the opposition and the guy who would rip off the button in the first place.

"Nice," Romano said.

The embassy was alerted that something was going down, but they weren't given details. The old Navy adage in play: Loose lips sink ships. Security had been beefed up, but the ambassador and his wife were back home in Indiana.

Washington had suggested the ambassador take a couple of weeks off.

So, on Day Three, there was agreement all around.

Operation Renegade was a go.

THE NIGHT of the mission was cool and clear. The moon was a sliver of ivory set in among fiery stars.

The Stealth-equipped Black Hawk crossed the Qarami border unobserved. When it reached the agreed-upon landing zone, STUD Unit One made a quick exit to the high desert floor. They were dressed in black and wore black balaclavas over their heads and faces.

The hoods served a double purpose. They masked identity of the wearer and added to the intimidation factor. In a raid, intimidation counted for a great deal.

They set out at their usual pace. Not slow, not fast, just a jog meant to get them where they were going without any effort. The only sound that stirred the silence was the soft crunch of booted feet on sand.

Halfway there, Dec called for a check. "Everybody good?"

The answers came back low and fast. Everybody was fine.

They reached the ruins of the ancient fort. It took a minute to locate the mouth of the old tunnel. And, yes, the entry was accessible, once they'd cleared away some debris.

Then they were in.

The tunnel had been carved out of the earth and lined with stone centuries before. It was a nasty place, wet and clammy with age. It was also was narrow. The guys from STUD One were big. Arms and bodies got scraped. Clothing got snagged. But breathing was the real problem. There was air, but it stank of dead creatures, of damp, of whatever had taken place here in years lost in the fog of time.

Still, nobody bitched. Bitching wasn't in STUD's code. Besides, the tunnel led straight to the basement, exactly as shown on the schematics. As for entry into the basement...The schematics had been unclear. Was it through a door? A door with a lock? Worst case scenario: Had the opening been bricked over? They had explosives with them, but the last thing they wanted was even a muffled bang.

Romano switched on a small LED flashlight.

Yes. It was a door. And it opened inward. He pushed against it. He could feel the wood start to give. Time and moisture had done their job. Two more shoves and it gave way.

They were in.

They paused just long enough to make a final check. Then Dec waved them on.

There wasn't much light, but there was enough to see by. It was clear the area wasn't used. There was slimy water on the stone floor, and the stink was almost as bad as in the tunnel.

And things scuttled over their feet.

"Rats," Spanos whispered.

Maguire, who had a thing about rodents, whispered back that they weren't rats, they were beetles.

"Beetles wearing size thirteen shoes," Sullivan whispered.

Soft chuckles. Hey, laughter was good, especially in tough situations.

For the next few minutes, it was text-book simple. Locate the service stairs. Done. Move quietly up the stairs to the first floor, hold for a three-count, then climb to the second floor. Done. Go down the corridor, no sounds, no noise. Done. Move slowly down the hall, weapons at the ready. Stop at the end where the corridor did a right turn that would lead to Uncle Shit's private chambers.

Dec held up his hand.

Everybody flattened themselves back against the wall.

He stepped out. Took a fast look.

As expected, there was an armed guard at the door.

Dec moved.

The guard saw him, but only at the last second. His hand went to his holster...

Too late.

Dec used his SOG-TAC knife. It was an efficient, fast, silent dispenser of death.

He caught the guard as he fell, eased him to the floor. Waved his guys forward. A quick nod at Olivieri, who reached for the doorknob. Dec and the others trained their HK MP7s on the door itself.

The knob turned. The door opened.

They were in an elaborate sitting room. Nobody there. Just silence. Wait. What was that? The sound of an impatient voice.

Quick hand signals. Romano dragged the guard's body inside and soundlessly shut the door. Dec pointed at him. Romano nodded. He would stay by the door. The others moved through the sitting room. Into a short hallway. Saw a half-open door ahead.

The bedroom.

Gilded walls. Canopied bed. And a tall, thin man, pacing restlessly across the silk carpet.

A smaller man sat on a low stool, needle and thread in his hand, a tuxedo jacket draped over his lap.

Uncle Shit. And the Freedom Fighter valet.

Uncle Shit snapped out what sounded like an insult. Dec looked at Alex, who'd studied languages and was fluent in several. Alex rolled his eyes and pointed to his watch.

Dec understood.

Uncle Shit was pissed off at how long the valet was taking to sew on a button.

The smaller man looked up and spoke. No translation needed. He was offering an apology—at least he was pretending to offer one.

Uncle Shit scowled. He swung towards the smaller

man. His tone was imperious and nasty—and Dec used the opportunity to make his move.

The dictator heard him, spun around, opened his mouth—

Dec jammed the butt of his rifle into the dictator's belly.

The guy grunted and doubled over. Dec caught him, jerked him upright, balled up his fist and punched him in the face. And again...

"Dude," Chay said. quietly "You have good reason to kill him—except the idea was to let the people of Qaram deal have him, remember? Hey, you don't want to let that happen, no sweat. We'll all be cool with it. Your call."

Dec was breathing hard. Not from exertion. From rage. But Chay's words got through. They had a deal with the Freedom Fighters, and he would honor it.

He moved back. Blanked his mind to the fury inside him.

"Yeah. Okay. Maguire. Secure the son of a bitch."

Aidan slapped duct tape over the dictator's mouth; Danny yanked his hands behind his back and zip-tied them together.

The smaller man stood up. He walked up to the unlawful ruler of Qaram, rose on his toes and spat full in his face.

"Your highness," he said coldly. "Your jacket is ready."

He dropped the jacket to the floor.

Dec grinned and patted the the valet on the shoulder. "Good job," he said. "Is anyone else here?"

The valet shook his head. "Only me."

"Will you be okay?"

The valet pulled a Glock that seemed to be almost as big as he was from under his jacket and pointed it at the dictator's head.

"I will be fine."

"I can see that," Dec said.

"Do not concern yourself with us, Lieutenant. We have planned for our liberation since the death of our true king. News of Cyrus's plans for war and for an alliance with the terrorist Amjad served only to make us move more quickly."

"Okay. Good. Just one more question. Do you know if Amjad is in his suite?"

The valet's face fell. "I am afraid that he is with our princess."

Dec went very still. He looked at Annie's uncle. "Anoushka had better be fine," he said through his teeth, "or I'll come back and kill you with my bare hands."

The uncle jerked his head up and down. He was white with fear; his eyes bulged with it. He said something, but the tape over his mouth rendered the words meaningless.

The valet, however, understood.

"He wants you to take him with you," he said. "He does not wish to remain here with me."

Dec smiled coldly. "I'll bet. Hell, no, pal. You're staying right here."

A soft, tinkling sound. They all looked down. The dictator was standing in a puddle of his own piss.

The valet chuckled. The men of Unit One grinned.

It was time to move on.

They moved quietly from the bedroom to the sitting room where Romano waited by the closed door. Dec nodded, and Nick cracked it open.

He peered up and down the corridor, then raised his hand and gave the all-clear.

They exited silently and, single file, made their way to where the corridor made another right angle turn.

Annie's suite was their next stop.

Dec raised his hand. All six STUDs flattened themselves against the wall. Dec leaned out. Took a fast look.

One guard, the same as at Uncle Shit's rooms.

Dec was quick and silent: a big predatory cat moving on its prey. He took the guard out with a killing chop to the side of the throat.

It was soundless and bloodless.

Then he reached for the doorknob.

"Wait!" Chay grabbed his shoulder. "Something," he whispered.

Nobody was going to argue. Chay Olivieri's sixth sense had been right too many times before.

Dec nodded. He pointed at Maguire and Spanos and shook his head. They were to hold back. He pointed to himself, then to Sullivan, Romano and Olivieri. Made a fist. Showed one finger. Two fingers. Three fingers...

He flung the door open.

"Lieutenant Sanchez, I presume," Altair Amjad

said in perfect English. "We have been waiting for you."

Six men stood in a semi-circle. Amjad stood in its center of the semi-circle, holding an AK47. It was pointed at Dec, but that didn't matter.

What mattered was that he had his other arm around Annie. She was drawn tightly back against him.

She was his shield.

Annie whispered Dec's name. He felt a rush of relief. She was okay. He wanted to tell her he loved her. That she was going to be fine. But to make that promise come true, he knew he could afford no distractions.

He reached up and yanked off his hood. "Amjad. Let the woman go."

The terrorist laughed, his teeth a flash of white against his thick salt-and-pepper beard.

"The woman? Do you mean my bride? Do not be foolish, Lieutenant. Why would I let her go after all I have gone through to claim her?"

"She isn't your bride, she's your captive."

"A technicality. Once we are married, she will change her mind." He chuckled and hoisted Annie to her toes. "Women love me, Lieutenant. And if they do not love me at first, I assure you that they learn to do so."

Jesus. Annie was trembling. Her face was white. Dec forced himself to concentrate on Amjad.

"Are you such a coward that you would hide behind a woman?"

"Are you such a fool that you believe such childish words would deter me?" The terrorist's brazen smile vanished. "Do you think anything you might say would have any meaning for me? I have not forgotten that you ambushed my men and slaughtered them. I owe you for that."

"An interesting viewpoint, Amjad. We defeated them after they attacked us."

Amjad narrowed his eyes. "Enough of this nonsense. Tell your men to put down their weapons. You too, Lieutenant."

"Do you know what a standoff is, Amjad?"

"Do you think I will not give the order for my men to kill you all? Do you think I am fool enough to believe that you, any of you, would fire at me when this woman you want stands in front of me?. Put down your weapons or this will not end well for her or for you."

"Don't do it, Declan," Annie said frantically. "He'll kill you."

Dec knew she was right. If he and his men put down their guns, they'd be shot dead. As for letting Annie be shot—the terrorist would do that too. Amjad was an egomaniacal barbarian, capable of anything.

Christ, he was helpless! All he could do was drop his rifle and then launch himself at Amjad in the desperate hope he could somehow save Annie...

"Ohhh..."

The cry had come from Annie.

"Be quiet, woman," Amjad snarled.

But she cried out again, gasping as if she couldn't

breathe, grabbing his arms with both hands as she began sliding down his body.

"Dammit," Amjad barked. "Stand up!"

Annie had gone limp. She was falling, dragging her captor down with her, and the terrorist let go of his rifle and wrapped both arms around her in a desperate effort to keep her upright.

Dec and his men leaped forward.

Dec let go of his own rifle, grabbed Amjad's and clubbed him in the face with its stock. Chay, Nick, Alex, Aidan and Danny were all over Amjad's men, rifle stocks swinging, knives out and flashing.

It was over in seconds.

Three of the terrorists were dead. Three were unconscious. The STUD operatives worked quickly, slapping duct tape over the mouths of the unconscious men, then binding their hands and feet with plastic restraints.

Dec reached for Annie.

But she had already scrambled upright. And she was...

Laughing?

Or crying. Or maybe doing a little of each.

"Annie?"

"I'm fine," she gasped. "I'm fine! Do I get an academy award for that performance or not?"

Dec figured what she'd get was either a kiss for bravery or a spanking for pulling such a dangerous stunt.

"Dammit, Anoushka, he could have killed you!"

"But he didn't," she said, and as he laughter turned

to soft sobs, Dec decided that for now, a kiss—a quick one—would have to do.

Amjad was down on his hands and knees, blood streaming from his broken nose. Chay had his Glock pressed to Amjad's forehead.

Dec kicked him in the side.

"Get up!"

Amjad raised his head. "You will regret this," he snarled. "You and your dissolute dogs will—"

Dec grabbed him by the nape of his neck and hauled him to his feet. He punched him in the gut. Air exploded from Amjad's lungs. It felt so good to hit the bastard that Dec drew back his fist and did it again.

"Declan," Annie said, "don't kill him. He would kill you, but you're better, so much better than he is."

Dec took a long, hard breath. Then he stepped back. They could debate how much better he was another time. Right now, she had reminded him that his mission was to bring the terrorist in alive.

Sometimes, doing your duty was tough.

Annie put her hand on his arm. He reached for her and drew her to him. He wanted to keep her like this forever, to tell her how much he loved her.

Instead, he looked at Amjad, hands bound, mouth taped, nose broken and bloodied. "All dressed up and ready to go," he said.

The others grinned.

"Okay," Dec said, pulling on his balaclava. "We're out of here."

"We leaving the three sleeping beauties?"

"Yeah. A little bonus for the Freedom Fighters."

The reverse trip was quick and smooth.

Danny went first, checking the corridor, then signaling it was clear. Nick and Chay went next, holding Amjad between them. Then Alex. Then Annie. Then Aidan, with Dec last.

No problems to the service stairs. None to the basement. One last trip through the tunnel—Amjad balked and Alex had the pleasure of jabbing him with the business end of his HK MP7 to get him moving.

They emerged into the clear, welcome night air at the ruins of the fort.

Then it was a fast jog to where the Black Hawk waited. Once they were on board, Dec dropped a hood over Amjad's head, and the big bird lifted into the sky.

The STUD One operatives grinned, pulled off their balaclavas and exchanged high fives.

"Piece of cake," Nick said.

Annie was crying and laughing at the same time. "I love you all," she said. "You're all wonderful."

"Don't forget handsome," Chay said.

"And brave," Aidan added.

"And brilliant," Danny said.

Dec laughed along with them. Then he took Annie in his arms. The other guys looked at each other, then looked away.

"That was some stunt you pulled, Princess," Dec said softly.

Her response was just as soft. "Theater Workshop 101."

"What?"

"I took an acting class in college. I was awful."

"How could you be awful at anything?"

"I was." She touched his jaw. "We did two one-act plays. I was so bad in the first one that the prof assigned me to help paint sets instead of letting me act the second time around."

'Yeah, well, he should have seen your performance tonight." Dec kissed her. "You were perfect." He tilted her face up to his. "Honey. Are you sure you're okay?"

"I'm fine."

She wasn't fine. She was trembling. And Dec had never loved her more than he did at that minute.

He drew her against him. "I thought I'd never seen you again, Anoushka," he whispered.

He felt her tears against his neck. "I love you, Declan. I'll always love you."

He kissed her, kissed her again. Then he looked at the men for whom he would willingly give his life and grinned.

"All right, you clowns. It's safe to turn around."

The guys swung towards them. "Didn't want to see a sloppy scene straight out of a chick flick," Chay said.

They all smiled.

And Dec and Annie knew that, at long last, they were on the journey that would be the start of their new life.

EPILOGUE

The debriefing took several days.

First there were the STUD debriefings, conducted by James Black.

Next came other debriefings: First a guy from State, then a woman from the DOD, followed by a colonel—not Stuart, who had not been heard from again—who represented the Joint Chiefs of Staff. A guy with a big smile and empty eyes flashed a badge none of them recognized and said he'd explain who he was, but then he'd have to kill them. Everybody laughed. Nobody asked for a further explanation. There was a pair of studious types from the CIA and a woman who chewed her nails from the NSA. A trio of intense-looking, intense-sounding guys from the alphabet-soup agency that oversaw STUD rounded out the cast of characters

After five days, the men of STUD One were all talked out.

The Secretary of State flew in from Washington to

meet with Annie. She had a phone call from the same city.

It provided the one light moment in a hard week.

"Princess Anoushka," a somewhat familiar voice said, "this is the President."

"Give me a break," Annie replied. "Who are you? And which guy in Dec's unit put you up to this?"

It turned out the call really was from the President. It took a couple of minutes until Annie was convinced, and then she did a lot of babbling to apologize. Fortunately, the President found her reaction amusing.

At last, the questions came to an end.

Operation Renegade was officially over.

So was the reign of Cyrus of Qaram. There'd been a trial and he'd been sentenced to life in prison.

Altair Amjad, the Deliverer, had been swallowed by the justice system. Some kind of justice system, at any rate. The last Dec heard of him was from Black, who said not to quote him, but the word was that the badass terrorist was in a badass place and singing like a canary.

Now, all that remained was what Dec worried might be an even tougher operation.

Annie loved him. He loved her. She'd said she wanted to spend her life with him. That was what he wanted too.

So far, so good.

But exactly how did two people manage that when one was a Special Ops warrior and the other was a princess?

"She isn't a princess anymore," Chay said over

beers one night at the LZ. Annie and his wife, Bianca, had gone to the ladies' room. "Bianca says Annie's working with an international children's aid program."

Dec nodded. "She is."

"My money's on you guys. You'll figure it out."

"Yeah," Dec said, all the doubt in the world in that *yeah*. He made a couple of circles on the table top with the wet bottom of his beer bottle. "Still, how do I know she hasn't thought it over and decided it's just gonna be impossible?"

"Thought what over?" Chay said. "Have you actually proposed to her yet?"

Dec shrugged. "No. Not yet. I mean, I just don't know how she'll respond..."

"How who will respond to what?" Annie said, as she slid into the booth next to him and nuzzled her face against his shoulder.

Dec looked stricken.

"How—how you guys will respond to the idea of pizza at the little Italian place up the road from here." Chay said.

Bianca sighed. "My favorite restaurant."

It was, indeed. It was Chay's too. The little Italian place was where Bianca and Chay had had their fist date. A date that had started off as awful and had ended in hot sex on the beach...

They drove to the restaurant, Chay and Bianca on his Harley, Dec and Annie in his lovingly restored Pontiac Trans Am.

They ordered Chianti, antipasti, and four different kinds of pasta—but nobody's attention seemed on the food. Chay and Bianca kept looking at each other in way that said *Do you remember that night*? Dec and Annie couldn't keep their hands off each other. When their waiter came to clear away all the food they'd left untouched and asked if they wanted dessert, Chay and Dec said "No!"

"No, thank you," Bianca and Annie added, because they were inevitably polite, even when each woman couldn't wait to be alone with her guy.

They parted company at the door. Bianca and Chay went in one direction; Annie and Dec headed for his cottage on the beach, where they'd been living together ever since Dec had brought her back from Qaram.

They kissed when Dec turned off the Trans Am.

Kissed again on their way to the front door.

Kissed again inside the dark cottage.

Dec took a deep breath. "Anoushka. I have to talk to you."

She nodded. "I have to talk to you too, Declan."

His heart sank. What did that mean? He wanted to ask, but he couldn't work up the courage. Firefights were easier than this.

He raised her chin, kissed the tip of her nose.

"Okay," he said, hoping he didn't sound as worried as he felt. "How about I open a bottle of wine and we take it outside? Take a walk on the beach? How's that sound?"

"Sure. That sounds great."

He nodded.

She nodded.

Then he thought, okay, enough was enough.

"Annie," he blurted, "my Anoushka, I love you. I adore you. I know there are a hundred reasons you could say no, but—but—"

"Are you asking me to marry you, Lieutenant?"

Dec was finding it difficult to breathe. "Yes," he said. "I am."

Annie smiled into his eyes. "I thought you'd never ask."

Dec swallowed hard. "Was that a yes?"

"It was absolutely a yes," she said gently. "Why would you have any doubts?"

"Anoushka." Dec cupped her face in his hands. "I have a job that's kind of crazy."

"You have a career, my love, that changes the lives of people in need of your help."

"And you're accustomed to a different kind of life."

"Yes," she said softly, "I am." She turned her face and kissed his palm. "I'm accustomed to the life I led when I was here, with you, as Annie Stanton. I want that life again—and I want it forever. You. Two kids. A dog. Maybe a couple of cats..."

Declan grinned as he gathered his princess into his arms.

"How about we plan the wedding first?"

She smiled. "An excellent idea."

"We'll have the ceremony wherever you choose. And a big party—"

Her Royal Highness, the Princess Anoushka, put her hand lightly over her lover's mouth.

"I'd like to have the ceremony on our beach. The party, too. Just our guys from Unit One."

"Our guys," Dec said, loving the sound of that.

"Well, and their dates. No date for Chay. I mean, Bianca—his wife will be his date. I've asked her to be my matron of honor. And we'll want your Captain Black, of course. Does he have a wife? And we won't leave out any of your friends who aren't in Unit One. Certainly not. And, oh, your parents, Declan! I can't wait to meet them. And—what's the name of that friend of yours who left the service? Tanner. That's it. Tanner. And his wife. Alessandra. She's Bianca's sister, isn't she? And—"

"Wait. Back up a little." Declan was laughing. "You already asked Bianca to be your matron of honor?"

"Yes. Well, I knew you'd get around to proposing sooner or later. And if you hadn't..." Annie smiled. "I was going to give you one more week, and then I intended to pop the question myself."

Declan shook his head. "How did I ever get so lucky?" he said softly. "To find you. To have you fall in love with me..."

"Any woman would fall in love with you, Lieutenant Sanchez."

Declan linked his hands in the small of Annie's back.

"Really," he said.

"Of course." She leaned back in his embrace and fluttered her lashes. "You're handsome. And brave. And strong. And smart."

He laughed. "That's all?"

"Well," She said coyly, "there's more…"

She leaned forward, stood on her toes and whispered in his ear.

Declan growled as he swept her into his arms. And Annie laughed and looped her arms around her lover's neck as he carried her through their cottage, through their bedroom, to their bed.

And to the glorious future that stretched out before them.

DEAR READER

Dear Reader:

I hope you enjoyed the story of Declan and Annie. I have to admit, there were times I got a little weepy as I wrote it and other times I laughed out loud. It would be wonderful to know you had a similar reaction.

If you haven't yet read POWER, Book One of STUD, or PRIVILEGE, Book Two, be sure and go to my website, www.sandramarton.com, for information on where to get your copies.

As always, if you enjoy my stories, you can tell me so via email or via Facebook. And you might want to leave a brief review wherever you buy my books. Great reviews are the best advertisements in the world!

With love and all my very best wishes,

Sandra

P.S. Guess whose story is coming next? Nick Romano's! Nick's a really great guy, but he's kind of stuck in a time and place when guys viewed women as the weaker sex.

Man, is he in for a surprise...